"You were afraid you'd end up divorced like your folks."

"How did you know that?"

"Because I know you. I've watched you watch her. So you've faced your fears, and you're up to the challenge of living."

"Yes, but not with a bull rider."

"What happened to both of us adapting?"

"What if you die?" Her voice quivered. "Where does that leave me?"

"I could get hit by a truck anytime."

"Yes, but when you ride bulls, the odds are against you living to be an old man, and I'd very much like you to do that for me."

"I can probably count on one hand the cowboys who've been killed by bulls." Clay stopped the horse, gave her a sugar cube, and walked over to the fence. "Remember, I'm ten foot tall and bull proof." He moved in for a kiss.

She jumped down and backed away. "I won't stand around and watch you get yourself killed."

SHANNON TAYLOR VANNATTER is a stay-at-home mom, pastor's wife, and writer. When not writing, she runs circles in the care and feeding of her husband, Grant; their nine-year-old son; and their church congregation. Home is a central Arkansas zoo with two charcoal gray cats, a chocolate lab, and three dachshunds in weenie dog heaven. If given the chance to clean house or write, she'd rather write. Her goal is to hire Alice from *The Brady Bunch*.

Books by Shannon Taylor Vannatter

HEARTSONG PRESENTS

Don't miss out on any of our super romances. Write to us at the following address for information on our newest releases and club information.

Heartsong Presents Readers' Service
PO Box 721
Uhrichsville, OH 44683

Or visit www.heartsongpresents.com

Rodeo
Dust

Shannon Taylor Vannatter

Heartsong Presents

In memory of my father-in-law, Louis Vannatter, a Southern Baptist pastor for over forty years in the San Antonio, Texas, area until he went to be with the Lord. We had lots of wonderful Texas visits, and I thank him from the bottom of my heart for the awesome gift of his son.

I appreciate DeeDee Barker-Wix, director of sales at the Cowtown Coliseum, for answering numerous questions over several months. I also appreciate Joe Hubb Baker—the Texas Kid—for his impromptu interview. I'd like to thank Aubrey City Hall secretary, Nancy Trammel-Downes, and Main Street Committee member, Deborah Goin, for sharing their knowledge of Aubrey's Peanut Festival. DeeDee and Nancy went above the call and critiqued a few scenes.

A note from the Author:
I love to hear from my readers! You may correspond with me by writing:

Shannon Taylor Vannatter
Author Relations
PO Box 721
Uhrichsville, OH 44683

ISBN 978-1-61626-724-7

RODEO DUST

All scripture quotations are taken from the King James Version of the Bible.

Our mission is to publish and distribute inspirational products offering exceptional value and biblical encouragement to the masses.

PRINTED IN THE U.S.A.

one

"Ew!" Rayna Landers's spike-heeled boot skidded in a huge pile of manure. Double doors, a hundred feet away, beckoned. At last, the final barn, lined with bored-looking Longhorns, on the endless, roller-coaster-rideless evening at the State Fair of Texas.

Captivated cowboys, cowgirls, and mini versions of both surveyed the cattle. The only place she wanted to see beef was in the form of filet mignon topped with mushroom sauce at Morton's Steakhouse.

A huge russet-colored bull glared at her through a rail barrier that surely couldn't contain the monster. Unmoving. Unblinking. Maybe he'd read her mind. He pawed at the sawdust under an enormous hoof with clear intentions of pulverizing her.

Despite the warmth of the late September evening, a chill seeped into her bones. She turned away from the massive beast and lunged for the safety of the nearby exit.

She looked back, certain the creature would surge through the fence and run her under. Something solid stopped her flight. She yelped and muscled arms caught her.

"Sorry, ma'am. Didn't see you coming." He stood well over six feet with eyes so green they almost glowed. Even with her at five feet nine and wearing heels, he still had a few inches on her. The requisite black hat, sitting at the perfect angle, couldn't quite restrain his raven curls. The cleft in his chin deepened with each heart-stopping smile.

While his looks gave her heart an erratic rhythm, his hands on her forearms felt safe, steady.

Step away from the cowboy.

Her feet took the mental hint, and she tried to wipe the muck off her heel in a patch of grass. She gulped for fresh air, but the smell of the stockyards persisted.

"Are you all right?"

"Fine. It was stuffy in there." Downtown Dallas had never before reeked like this. At least, not in her experience.

"It does get warm in there. At least our fair is always in the fall, so we don't cook."

A beautiful Palomino stood next to a trailer, its pale golden coat gleaming and platinum tail swishing. Rayna stepped closer, drawn by the mare's beauty. Years ago, her city-dwelling father had taken her to several dude ranches, but she hadn't gotten this close since. The Palomino was her favorite color, and her fingers itched to touch the creamy hide.

"You can pet her if you want, ma'am."

"She's yours?" Gorgeous man, gorgeous horse.

"Name's Clay Warren. This is Buttercream. Raised her myself, but I let my mama name her." He stroked the horse as he regaled Rayna with a list of the mare's awards and ribbons.

Though enchanting, the horse didn't hold her attention, but the man certainly did. Buttercream whinnied as if she knew their focus had shifted away from her.

Clay winked. "Guess she doesn't like competition from beautiful ladies."

Her gaze flew back to the horse and warmth crept over her. The cowboy's boldness jangled her nerves, yet she liked it. She tucked a long strand of hair behind her ear.

"Oops." The cowboy looked past her and winced. "Hope your husband didn't hear that. Sorry, I didn't see a wedding ring."

She turned. Her brother stalked toward them, a disgusted scowl marring his features. She frowned. Surely he and Gabby were getting along okay. They were perfect for each other.

"Rayna, where did you go?"

"Where's Gabby?"

"She's coming." Adam's stare riveted on Clay.

Why did he have such an annoying tendency to be overprotective of her? "Okay Adam, you drag me here as a guise to date my best friend, and then you abandon her. Not a good plan."

Adam's jaw clenched. "I don't think this stranger needs to know that."

"Clay Warren." A confused frown flawed his forehead. "I was just acquainting the lady with my horse."

Wondering who Adam was, no doubt, all dark hair and eyes like their dad, while Rayna's auburn hair and amber eyes must have come from the absentee mom.

"This is my brother"—Rayna searched the crowd behind them for Gabby—"who is supposed to be impressing my best friend with his plans for a future ranch. Adam, you'd better go find her."

"I think I'll stay right here." Adam crossed his arms over his chest.

"Rayna wanted to pet my horse. Go ahead." Clay took her hand and smoothed it down the mare's velvety muzzle.

His calloused grip swept warmth up her arm.

"*We* need to go find Gabby." Adam's tone was glacial.

Apparently he noticed when Clay's hand lingered over hers a little too long. Rayna sighed. She didn't want Gabby mad at Adam, and he obviously wouldn't budge without her.

"Your horse is exquisite." Not wanting to let the cowboy go, her eyes locked with his again. "Thank you for letting me visit with her."

"Anytime, ma'am. Nice meeting you." He tipped his hat and offered his business card. "Do you have a last name, pretty lady?"

"Landers." Her insides pooled like melted butter. She'd never experienced such blatant flirtation—especially in the face of her brother's resentment.

Clay held the card longer than necessary. His fingers grazed hers.

Adam touched her elbow.

Clay let go, and she quickly stuffed his card into her pocket.

"It was nice to meet you." She managed to get the words out as Adam steered her away.

Gabby exited the barn.

Rayna hurried to meet her, careful where she stepped. Nothing about this part of the fair impressed her. Not hopscotching over pile after pile of animal waste. Not swatting at swarms of flies. Not the stench of farm animals, the stomach-turning greasy food, or the blare of country music.

But there was the cowboy. He probably liked roller coasters.

"There you are." Gabby frowned at Adam. "I turned around, and you were gone."

"Adam was worried about me." Rayna shrugged. "I needed some air."

"Your asthma." Adam blew out a sigh and steered them toward the food booths. "I didn't even think about that."

"It was nothing like that. I haven't had an attack in months."

Lord, please don't let my matchmaking efforts fall apart now. During the course of the evening, she'd definitely become a third wheel. If it worked out between Adam and Gabby, this dismal outing would all be worth it.

"I'm sorry, Gabby. I had to save Rayna from a cowboy."

Rayna laughed. "I didn't need saving. He was nice."

"You don't know how cowboys are, little sister. They only want one thing and expect all women to fall at their feet."

"Oh come on, Adam." Gabby stopped, propping her hands on both hips. "That's rather a blanket statement."

"He gave her his number." Adam's jaw clenched.

"Really?" Gabby grinned. "Rayna's a big girl, and if she wants to call him she can. When it starts getting serious, she'll dump him. So you don't have anything to worry about." She patted Adam's arm.

"Hey," Rayna said, frowning, "I resent being talked about as if I'm not here. Why does everyone think just because I happen to be female my sole purpose in life should be to land a husband and have babies?" She hugged herself.

"Gabby didn't mean to step on any feminist toes."

"And I'm not a feminist. I happen to enjoy my career. What's wrong with dreaming of getting a promotion and buying a town house?"

"Nothing. Just sounds kind of. . .lonely." Gabby looked past her. "How about some cotton candy?"

Rayna turned to see a man with his hand stuck through a plastic dome. In a big silver tub, he twirled blue fluff onto a stick. Her stomach churned. Eat the sweet treat with the sickening aroma of horse manure burned into her nostrils?

"We haven't even eaten supper yet." Adam checked his watch. "It's almost six."

"I'm not really hungry." Rayna's stomach growled a protest at her ruse. "Y'all go somewhere for dinner. I'll take a cab home."

"You are not taking a cab." Gabby shook her head. "We'll take you home, and then Adam and I will get a bite to eat. We can even come back here. If that's okay with you, Adam." She flashed a shy grin.

Adam nodded like a bobble head. "Fine by me."

Rayna grinned. The evening wasn't a total loss. Not to mention meeting Clay.

They maneuvered slowly through the press of the vast multitude clad in western wear and faded denim. Black jeans and teal sweater marked her—outsider.

As they exited the gate, the giant cowboy statue waved. "Howdy folks," Big Tex boomed.

Rayna jumped.

They trekked the quarter of a mile to Adam's black SUV. Rayna hurried to get in the back, forcing Gabby to sit up front.

He started the engine and backed out. A pickup let them into the flow of traffic, and Rayna waved her thanks.

"I'm really glad you came, Gabby." Adam cleared his throat. "I had a great time up until the cocky hayseed flirted with my sister. Maybe you and I can come back tonight and next weekend, too?"

ᨀ

Rayna hurried to her condo. Adam's engine rumbled nearby as Gabby walked her to the door.

"Thanks for inviting me tonight." Gabby grinned. "Adam is great. I don't know why I never saw that at the office."

"I told you." Rayna unlocked the red door.

"You never told me he dreamed of owning a ranch someday, just like where I grew up."

"I wanted him to tell you." Rayna shooed her away. "Now scoot. He's waiting."

"Call the cowboy."

"What could we possibly have in common?"

"I probably should stay out of it, but I'm not good at that, so here goes. Just because both sets of grandparents, a couple of aunts and uncles, and your parents divorced, it doesn't mean you shouldn't get married. Just because your mom left"—Gabby took a deep breath—"it doesn't mean you'll end up like her."

Rayna swallowed hard. There it was, her biggest fear, spoken out loud. The thing she'd never even found the courage to voice herself. The thing she thought she'd kept hidden.

She gripped the cold doorknob tighter.

"You're not your mother. You're the most loyal person I know. I'm telling you this because I love you." Gabby pecked Rayna's cheek. "And I want you to be happy. You have the heart to be a great wife and a great mom."

But did she have the stick-to-itiveness? Even if she did, could she find a man who'd hang in there with her?

The two women hugged.

"Call the cowboy."

"I don't call men."

Gabby rolled her eyes. "If it's not him, somebody else. Go to the singles class at church. Stick around long enough to get serious. Live happily ever after. Doctor's orders." Gabby wagged a finger and turned away.

"See you at work." Rayna stepped inside and locked the door then leaned against it. Kicking off her boots stirred up a fresh whiff. She picked them up by two fingertips and deposited them in the laundry room.

Sock footed, she checked her caller ID and fished the business card from her pocket. It gave the name of his dude ranch in Aubrey, number included. What would she do with a cowboy? Definitely not her type.

She hurried to the kitchen then hesitated, hand suspended over the trash. Just drop it. But her fingers wouldn't comply. She stuffed the card into her junk drawer.

Her stomach rumbled. Ebony granite countertops held red small appliances waiting to whip up gourmet fare. But her recent haute cuisine class and all the gadgets didn't help her work up any enthusiasm to cook for only one. Except for the cappuccino machine, she rarely used them unless she took supper to her dad. Preparing food for herself, no matter how elaborate, just wasn't any fun.

She checked her watch. Maybe it wasn't too late. She picked up the handset and dialed. It rang twice.

"Hello?"

"Hey Daddy, have you eaten yet? I thought I might bring something over."

"Sweetheart." His voice filled with regret. "That sounds wonderful, but. . .I have plans."

Plans? The lump in her throat swelled. She ran her fingers over the polished, smooth surface of the countertop. Plans with a woman? "Okay, maybe some other night."

"I'm sorry, sweetheart."

Rayna nodded. "No problem. I just thought if you were free—have a nice evening."

She leaned back against the cabinet and wrapped her arms around herself. Her dad never had plans. When he left his psychology practice, he always went home. Alone.

It must be a woman. Which was fine. But. . . "Lord, please don't let him get hurt. He's been hurt enough."

❧

Close to midnight, Clay finished his forty-minute commute to the ranch with the trailer rattling behind.

"I sure liked her, Lord, but I'm always a sucker for redheads, and there's more to a woman than beauty. I could look her up, give her a call, find out what she's all about." He sighed. "I know You've got the perfect lady for me; just help me find her.

I'm ready. Past ready."

At the barn, he backed up the Silverado and unloaded Buttercream. The *clop-clop* of restless hooves sounded in the stalls. He jogged toward the house as neighs and nickers echoed through the crisp night air. Ah, the sounds of home.

He stepped inside, hung his corduroy jacket on a wooden peg behind the door, and stopped to turn off a light in the office. The scent of pine needles greeted him from a candle burning on the cedar coffee table. Mama sat at the desk, her graying auburn hair aflame in the glow of the lamp with a Holstein shade she'd gotten him last Christmas. Dad snored from the suede couch.

"Hey Mama, what are y'all doing here so late?"

"Earning my keep as a good little bookkeeper. Paying bills—working the numbers."

He stood behind her and massaged her tense shoulders. "Feels like you've been at it too long."

"Oooh, that's good. Up along the side of my neck."

He kneaded his thumbs along numerous knots. "How's it looking?"

"The Horizon Finals purse sure helped. Oooh. Oooh, right there." She tilted her head to the left. "That alone will take care of the vet, repairs, and get you well ahead on the loan payments. Probably pay off the new fence and horse trailer, too."

"Where does that leave the hands? Guess I better win CBR World, too."

"Now, don't go putting too much pressure on yourself." She turned to face him. "You've done great this season. Especially after last year's injury. God will work it out. You'll see. Business will pick up soon."

When? He ran his fingers through his hair. "God might have opened up a path to help it along. My sponsor called me today. They want to do a media blitz with me hawking their clothing line."

"Yee-haaa!" She jumped up to hug him.

"I really don't wanna do it." He winced. "It's like a modeling gig."

"But Clay, you going high profile might put the ranch on the map."

"What? What's going on?" Dad blinked then settled. Seconds later, he snored again, the big gasping kind.

"Why's Dad so tired?" Clay frowned at the older version of himself.

"He broke the gray stallion today."

Or the gray stallion broke Dad. The living legend that was his father lay deep in slumber. His six-foot-four frame folded and kinked on the too-short couch, feet dangling over the end. Four-time National Circuit Champ. Even if Clay trounced the record with five CBR World titles, he could never fill those size thirteens.

Mama saved her file and turned away from the computer. "Tell me more about Cowboy Western Wear's plans."

"I haven't agreed yet." Dad never had to be a spokesmodel to make ends meet.

"It's your decision, son." She picked at a red fingernail. "But keep in mind, if you turn them down, they might bail on sponsoring you. A tidy little sum like the World purse would keep all your employees."

"That's the only reason I'm considering it. Go to bed. No sense driving home so late." *And there are plenty of empty rooms here.*

She kissed his cheek. "It's not far."

"Take Dad with you before he gets a crick in his neck for church tomorrow."

&

Nothing had gone right today with the new ad campaign. Rayna jammed her key into the condo lock and it clicked open. Why did Monday always have to be Monday? Tossing her keys on the countertop, she checked her caller ID then did a double take.

Warren Dude Ranch, 4:23 p.m. How did he get her number?

"Okay, if I call now, it's not like I made the first move. I'd simply be returning his call."

She dug his business card out of the drawer with a grin.

"Great. He's got me talking to myself."

She tossed the card on the black coffee table and lit a cinnamon candle. Plopping on the crimson leather sofa, she picked up the novel she'd been reading. But the description of the hero made her think of Clay. She put the book down and channel surfed in vain for something decent on TV then clicked it off.

She paced the condo, straightening strategically placed throw pillows and setting three magazines in a just-so fan shape. The card beside them beckoned. She grabbed her cell phone. Her hands shook as she dialed the number.

two

"Howdy, Warren Dude Ranch," a man's voice greeted her, but not the one she wanted to hear.

"This is Rayna Landers. Is Mr. Clay Warren in?" Her heart would surely beat out of her chest.

"Sorry, you just missed him. He'll be out of town till Thursday. Can I help you?"

A sigh emanated from deep within, and her lungs seemed to deflate. "Uh, no, that's okay. I wanted to book a vacation."

"I can help you with that."

"Thanks, but I need to double-check my schedule anyway. I'll call back."

Why was she so disappointed? Shoulders slumped, she trudged into her sleek kitchen and sought the solace of a cappuccino.

❧

Clay climbed out of the truck, stretched his arms high above his head, and rolled his neck from side to side. Crisp autumn air filled his lungs. A long couple of days at the Waller County Fair. A long four-hour drive home, but he'd networked with some big-time horse enthusiasts and impressed them with his stock.

Almost six. Eager for his own bed tonight, he might just turn in early. He left the hands to unload the trailer and headed toward the house.

Ben, his ranch hand/clerk, stood behind the polished cedar counter, the phone propped between his shoulder and ear. Sounded like a reservation. Maybe things were looking up, and he wouldn't have to do the modeling thing.

"Yes, thank you, sir." Keys clicked on Ben's keyboard, and he hung up. "Welcome home, Clay."

"Thanks. How are things here?"

"Good. We got two reservations for the weekend and another bite. Said she'd call back later. I wrote her number down for follow-up." Ben handed him several messages as the phone rang again.

The door to the private dining room opened. Dad looked more rested at least.

"Welcome home, son. Any nibbles?"

"I met with the ranch owner from Waco I told you about. I think he might buy some horses."

His dad clapped him on the back. "Here's hopin'."

Clay scanned through the messages as he turned toward the stairs. Rayna Landers? He stopped in midstride.

"What is it, son?" Dad frowned.

"Just an unexpected call."

"Good or bad?"

"Good. Definitely good." Clay took the stairs two at a time to his private office.

&

Rayna counted repetitions as she lifted free weights at the women-only health club. A vibration pulsed against her thigh and she jumped. Slightly out of breath, she set down the barbells and retrieved her cell from the pocket of her warm-up pants.

Clay. Her heart lodged in her throat.

She'd studied his business card enough to know the number. Sucking in a deep breath, she gathered all her frayed nerves and stepped into the deserted dressing room.

"Hello?"

"Hi. You called about booking a vacation." Clay's soft drawl set her pulse aflutter.

"This is Rayna Landers. Um. . .we met at the—"

"I remember, pretty lady. Amber eyes, copper hair, and not a freckle in sight. Rare for a redhead. You sound out of breath."

"I'm at the gym." Numerous mirrors lined the dressing room. Thank goodness he couldn't see her now with her sheen of sweat, melting makeup, and frazzled hair.

"Want me to call you back?"

"No, this is fine." *Stop sounding desperate.* She traced the phone with her fingertips and summoned up an all-business tone. "I'm planning a vacation soon and wanted to book a week at your ranch. Do you have any openings in the next month or so?"

"As a matter of fact, I do. How about we discuss the details over lunch?"

"Lunch?" With the cutest cowboy she'd ever seen? Could her traitorous pulse handle the heat?

"You're breaking my heart. Tell me you called for more than a vacation?"

"Well, I—" She smoothed damp tendrils away from her face.

"Come on. Have lunch with me. I'm tied up Friday and Saturday night with work, but I'm free Saturday. I called last week, but you weren't home."

"How did you get my home number?"

"Took my chances on the only R. Landers in the book and won. And when you called, Ben got your cell number off caller ID as a potential client. Deep down, I was hoping you were returning my call."

"Actually, I was, but I am interested in a vacation." *Eventually.*

"I'll bring my calendar to lunch."

Surely her erratic heart would leap out of her chest. "Okay. Where should we meet?"

"Meet? I'll pick you up."

"Tell me where to meet you."

"Ah, you don't trust me?"

She wanted to. "I never get in a man's car until we're acquainted well enough for me to decide whether he deserves my trust. Or not."

"Smart and pretty. Actually, I drive a pickup. Would you like to know in whom I place my trust?"

Her breath caught. "Are you saying you don't trust me?"

The deep timbre of his laughter sent a shiver over her. "I

think I could handle you, Rayna Landers. No, what I mean is, I'm a Christian. I trust Jesus Christ as my Lord and Savior. Does that help you to know whether I'm trustworthy or not?"

Never in her twenty-five years had she heard a man speak so boldly of his faith, other than her pastor.

"Are you still there?"

"Yes, I'm here." Her words came out breathless.

"You're not a Christian, are you?"

"No! I mean, yes." Rayna closed her eyes. Why did he fluster her so? She stopped pacing and perched on the arm of a taupe nail-head chair. "What I mean is, I'm a Christian, but I'd still rather meet you."

"Hmm. A Christian with trust issues. I reckon you're just using your beautiful head. A gal can't be too careful. What if I come to your place, and you follow my truck to where we're going?"

"Then you'd know where I live."

"I already know where you live. I looked you up in the book, remember?"

"Oh." Somehow she didn't feel threatened. Warmth curled through her stomach.

"Nine o'clock Saturday morning?"

"I thought you said lunch."

"I did, but on second thought, let's make a day of it. Do you like parades?"

"Why?"

"You don't have other plans, do you?"

"Well no, but—"

"Great, the parade starts at ten. Wear comfortable shoes." He hung up.

A parade? A day of it? Her finger hovered over the redial button. She should call him back and cancel. He'd offered lunch then roped her into a parade and the whole day. But she wouldn't mind spending a day with him. If he turned out to be a jerk, she'd have her car.

Such a contradiction. This man who'd shamelessly flirted

with her at the fair was a Christian.

On the way to the treadmill, she mentally scanned the inventory of her closet. *What do you wear on a date with a cowboy?*

✿

Feminine laughter echoed around Rayna as she shared lunch with her two coworkers at their favorite Dallas café, Maguire's. Every Friday they aired hopes and dreams. At their usual corner table, Rayna enjoyed her usual grilled-chicken salad with Italian vinaigrette as the server set their usual pitcher of Diet Coke in the middle of the gathering.

"No seriously, how do I let Adam know I'm interested?" Gabby set her glass down. "Should I wink at him?"

"Please don't." Kendra's voice dripped sarcasm.

Rayna speared a cherry tomato and popped it into her mouth. So good to see Gabby smiling again. She wanted Gabby and Adam together, but was it voyeuristic discussing her brother's budding relationship?

"Winking is so out." Kendra shook her head. "You've been out of the dating scene entirely too long."

Apparently, Kendra had never been on the receiving end of a cowboy's wink.

"Tell me Miss Expert, how do you let a guy know you're interested? What's the *in* way?" Gabby sipped her diet soda.

"Anything but winking. Look at him and smile; then glance away, and look again. Lick your lips. Tuck your hair behind your ear."

Rayna swallowed hard. *I tucked my hair behind my ear at the fair.*

"You're right," Gabby moaned. "I've been out of the loop for too long. Tucker and I dated for six months, and it's been that long since we broke up. I've lost my touch."

"No, you haven't." Rayna patted her friend's hand. "Adam likes you, and he'll get it no matter what you do. Even if you wink. Be up front with him, not all this silly, coy stuff."

"But what if he doesn't ask me out again?" Gabby fiddled with the edge of the tablecloth.

"He already has. He mentioned going to the fair again." Rayna took a deep breath and exhaled slowly. "Relax. If it's right, God will work it out."

"Here we go with the God stuff." Kendra rolled her eyes. "If it weren't for that God stuff, she'd still be with Tucker."

Rayna refolded her cloth napkin. Would their witnessing lunches ever get anywhere with Kendra? "Gabby did the right thing with Tucker. If he'd been the man she needed, he'd have stuck around."

"Oh that's just great—coming from the only other virgin I know. I don't get the two of you. Tucker loved you, Gabby. When a man loves a woman, sex is the natural progression of things. I'm surprised he stuck around as long as he did without it."

"If he really loved her, he'd have been willing to wait." Rayna traced the rim of her glass with her fingertip. "Till after the wedding."

"Couldn't they have skipped to the honeymoon? I mean, they would've gotten married later, so what's the difference?"

"Don't you see?" Gabby splayed both hands, palms up. "If I'd slept with him, maybe he wouldn't have ever married me, and even if he still wanted to, what if he died on the way to the church? The Bible teaches us that sex is a beautiful thing only to be shared between husband and wife."

Gabby wadded her napkin and dropped it on her plate. "Somewhere out there God has the perfect guy waiting for me."

"Maybe he's right down the hall." Rayna patted Gabby's hand again.

"So what's the other virgin doing this weekend? Singing in the choir?" Kendra smirked.

Don't let it show how her teasing grates on the nerves. "I do plan on going to church, but I'm not in the choir."

"Did you call him yet?" Gabby's eyes widened.

"Who?" Kendra's radar perked up.

Rayna stifled a wince. "This guy I met at the state fair."

Kendra waved her fork in the air. "Do tell. He gave you his number?"

"Just his business card." Rayna kept her tone light.

"Ooh, a businessman. What kind of business?" Kendra leaned forward.

"A dude ranch."

Kendra hooted. "A cowboy. You fell for a cowboy?"

"No, I didn't fall for him. I met him. Weren't you raised on a farm?"

"Yes, but I got over it." Kendra huffed an exaggerated sigh. "Some people simply insist on staying there. A cowboy. Did you call him?"

"It wasn't like that. Since I fell in love with his horse, he probably thought I might be interested in his dude ranch and gave me his card. End of story."

"Don't look now, but there are three great-looking guys at two o'clock checking us out." Kendra tucked a too-black strand with burgundy highlights behind her ear.

"Why can't women have lunch without being ogled?" Gabby rolled her eyes.

"You need to scan the merchandise before you go and get all high and mighty. One of these lookers might take your mind off of what's his name."

"Adam will do that for her." Rayna retrieved her pewter-colored handbag from under the table and stood. "We need to get back to work. We've got a campaign to develop."

Kendra's eyebrows rose. "Maybe we could use one of those perfect specimens for a model."

Gabby slung her bag over her shoulder. "You're incorrigible."

On the way to the car, Rayna tried to concentrate on the basketball shoe ad campaign instead of Clay Warren.

"Sorry about that," Gabby whispered. "Me and my big mouth."

It couldn't be helped now. "It's okay."

"She'll drive you nuts about it."

"I can tune her out." Rayna pushed the button on her key ring to unlock her silver sports car.

"Are you going to call him?"

"Actually, he called me. We have a date tomorrow." She

pressed her finger to her lips and glanced at Kendra already getting in the car. "Shhh."

❧

Clay's brake lights came on. Rayna scanned the speed limit sign and slowed her car. BUL PRUF, his license plate proclaimed. What was that supposed to mean? Probably the way it came out and not a personalization.

The city faded away. AUBREY, HORSE COUNTRY USA, a sign declared. Houses dotted the landscape back off the road. Children played in wide-open spaces. The life she could never have.

As they neared the center of town, heavy traffic marred the peacefulness. A large white church was the focal point of the small town. Ever After Chapel, the kind of picturesque church a girl would want to get married in. Why did her thoughts keep straying in that dangerous direction?

Clay's blinker came on. She followed his hunter-green truck into a parking lot.

He hurried to open the door for her. His jeans, western shirt, and boots didn't contrast too badly with her royal button-down blouse and dark denims.

He let out a long, slow whistle. "Did I mention you're beautiful?"

A blush heated her skin. "Thank you. Are you sure I'm dressed okay?"

"You're perfect. We'll have to walk this block to get there, but I didn't figure I could find two spaces any closer."

"Where is this place? What's the parade for?"

"This is our annual Peanut Festival. Aubrey grows peanuts and horses. It's always the first Saturday in October since 1986. All the proceeds go to buy books for the library."

Clay's hand engulfed hers, sending warmth up her arm. The same way his touch had affected her the first time they'd met. Hand in hand, they walked around the block in silence.

Booths lined a grassy open lot, displaying jewelry, crafts, local businesses, a variety of peanut products, and food. Only a few hat-free heads dotted the crowd of denim-clad men, women, and children milling about. A live band played country music from a small stage and children played games at some of the booths.

"The parade will start in a few minutes. Afterward, I thought we could check out the booths and eat lunch here, unless it's not your kind of place. All items sold here are handmade."

A quilt caught Rayna's eye. A complex pattern of gray swirls, black polka dots, and red paisley. Perfect for chilly evenings when she sat up to watch a late movie. Alone. She hurried to get a better look.

"The booths don't open until after the parade." Clay's grip tightened on her fingers. "They're just setting up."

"I want this quilt." Rayna ran her free hand over the soft fabric and intricate stitching.

"Hi, Abigail," Clay tipped his hat.

Rayna noticed the grandmotherly woman sitting in the booth, wearing a smile of accomplishment.

"It's lovely. You made this?"

"Yes, ma'am. Thank you."

"Can you hold it for me?" Clay pulled out his wallet.

"I'll pay for it." Rayna dug her money clip out of her pocket, whipped the bills out before he could, and passed them to Abigail.

The woman picked up the quilt. "I'll hold it under the counter, and you can pick it up after the parade."

"Thank you."

Clay pressed a hand to the small of Rayna's back. "The parade's starting."

A police car crept down the street with lights flashing. A dance troop followed in several single-file rows, hands on their hips, taking synchronized steps to the rhythm of a song.

"That looks fun. I wish I knew how to dance."

"Where's that risk taker?" he drawled close to her ear. "I could teach you the Texas Two-Step sometime."

She shivered and the twangy music she thought she loathed put a lump in her throat with its patriotic lyrics. Or maybe it was his nearness. Or the thought of dancing with him.

Somehow, as she and Clay oohed, laughed, and twanged through the parade, they didn't seem so different.

Could she find common ground with Clay?

What was she thinking? She could never entertain thoughts of common ground with anyone.

As the last float wrapped up the parade, Clay squeezed her hand and led her to the row of food booths. "Let's get something to eat, and then we'll get your quilt and look around."

Instead of surveying the neon menu, her gaze stayed on Clay.

He caught her staring, and once again, her sensitive skin betrayed her with familiar warmth.

"What?" One brow lifted.

She refocused on the menu. "I think I'll try the grilled chicken."

"You have to try the ribs."

"I do?"

"You don't have to, but you should. Do you like ribs?"

"Yes, but I think I'll stick with the chicken."

"Why, if you like ribs?"

"They're messy."

"Afraid a little barbecue sauce dripping down your chin might disgust me?"

Mischief danced in his eyes, and she laughed.

"As a matter of fact, I don't make a habit of eating messy finger foods in public." *Especially on a first date.*

"Well pretty lady, if you want chicken, order it. But if you'd like to have some fun, try the ribs. Surely you won't let me be the only one with barbecue sauce on my chin." He stuck his bottom lip out in a pout.

Instead of coming across comical, he looked quite. . . kissable.

Rayna swallowed hard. "You're on. Ribs it is."

"I knew it. You're a risk taker. I like that in a gal. Besides, they give you a wet wipe to mop up with after you're done."

Jittery and extremely self-conscious, she sat at a picnic table while he ordered, waited for their food, and paid.

Instead of sitting across from her, he sat beside her. Butterflies took flight in her stomach. He blessed the food, and she liked him even more.

Rayna tried to strip the meat from the bone with her plastic fork.

"Just dig in." Clay winked.

She sank her teeth into a juicy rib with sweet and tangy sauce dripping. "You were so right. These are the best ribs I've ever had. The meat is so tender it falls off the bone."

"You've got sauce on your chin."

She giggled as he used his napkin to wipe it off for her.

After the ribs, turtle cheesecake on a stick made Rayna's nervousness ebb.

"So, you own a dude ranch. What else do you do?"

"I teach Sunday school, and I'm a church usher. I don't curse or drink."

This cowboy stood behind his convictions. Impressive.

"And I ride bulls."

A shudder moved through her.

"You cold?"

"I'm fine." For some reason, ever since she'd seen that huge bull at the fair, the mere thought of it gave her a deep sense of foreboding. She shrugged it off. "Isn't that dangerous?"

"It can be. But darlin', don't you know? I'm ten foot tall and bull proof."

The drawled endearment put some heat back in her flesh. "What else do you do?"

"Ride broncs."

"Is there a rodeo tonight?"

"Rodeo is a year—"

"Round sport in Texas. Do you win?"

"At the moment, I'm at the top of the standings in bull riding. I got into the big-time rodeo just to buy the dude ranch, but somewhere along the way, I got addicted."

She wanted to ask what could be addicting about a bull

but decided she'd shown enough ignorance of his sport.

He took a swig of root beer. "Have you ever been to a rodeo?"

She shook her head.

"Even as a kid? Watched one on TV?"

"My dad and brother hate rodeos, and I don't watch much TV. When I do, I hate sports so much I put a block on those channels."

A perplexed frown marred his forehead. "Tell me about being an ad exec."

"I was still in college when Adam got me hired on at Bradley & Associates as a photographer. After I got my visual arts degree, I climbed the ladder to art director."

"And from the way your eyes just lit up, you love it."

"It's fun taking a product or a personality very few people have heard of, coming up with the right angle, and watching the public embrace it."

"Do you have a card? I might be able to use your services. My sponsor's wanting some publicity."

"Sure." She dug around in her purse, passed him a card, and glanced at her watch. "It's after one."

"Do you turn into a pumpkin at two?" He winked.

She felt the blush. Where had the time gone? "I'm eager to get my quilt and see what else I can find."

He held out his hand. "Allow me."

Allow him to swagger his way under her skin? Her fingers slipped into his.

&

A few hours later, Clay helped her carry her purchases. Several items of jewelry, a throw pillow to go with her quilt, and a miniature pulpit decorated with lace and ribbon with a small open Bible on top. The perfect Christmas gift for Gabby.

As they crossed the street and headed around the block, early October evening air sent a shiver over her. Or maybe it was Clay.

"I wish we could stay longer, but I've got the rodeo

tonight." He put his arm around her shoulders, stirring the erratic rhythm of her heart to a frenzy. Her mind went blank.

Think of something to say. Anything to get her mind off his nearness. How come every time they were alone and close, she went mute?

They stopped beside her car.

She held her breath when he brought the back of her hand to his lips. A tingling sensation moved up her arm.

"What's your brother got against me?"

"It's not you." But Adam's ire did seem a little more extreme than usual. She leaned against the driver's side door. "He's a bit overprotective."

"I think there was more to it." He kicked at something unseen with the toe of his boot.

"You two should have a lot in common." *Unlike us.* "He wants to retire someday and own a ranch. I'm city through and through."

"I'm more interested in you. When can I see you again?"

"Are you sure you want to?"

"Our lifestyles are different, but opposites attract." He aimed another mind-spinning grin at her.

"Yes, but there should be some things in common, too."

"We're both Christians. We share the same values."

"The most important thing. But what else?" She tipped her bottled water to her lips.

"Let's be right up front about things. I'm looking for a wife."

three

Rayna sputtered and almost choked. She was getting used to his boldness, but this line of conversation messed with her pulse. "That was certainly right up front. Do I have to answer now or can I think about it?"

"I don't mean in the next few months or even six. I just want you to know my intentions. I believe dating is a way for us to find a partner for life. I'd like to have the basic 2.5 children and live in a cabin in the woods a few acres away from the dude ranch. But how do you have 2.5 children? Just make it three."

He'd named off everything she couldn't dream of. The distant twang of the music got louder for a moment then faded again.

"How about you? Are you looking to get serious?"

As her heart clamored in her chest, she cleared her throat. "Actually, I don't want to get married. I'd like to concentrate on my career, upgrade to a town house nowhere near the woods, and I don't want children."

"You don't?" A confused frown furrowed his brow as if she'd suddenly sprouted extra arms. He gazed up into the sky. "Why not?"

"I don't know." She shrugged, trying to sound casual. "I just never have. When I was a kid and the neighborhood girls played house with their dolls, I never got into that."

"Then why did you agree to today?"

His charm, his eyes, his swagger. "I don't mind dating."

"Just so it doesn't go no further. What about when you're old and gray? Think your career will keep the loneliness at bay?"

She swallowed the fears clogging her throat. "I'm only twenty-five. Maybe I'll be ready to settle down by the time

I'm coloring my hair." The lie tasted bitter. "I guess this isn't going to work, huh?"

He dropped her hand. "Guess I shouldn't invite you to the rodeo."

A tense silence shrouded them, and she got into her car. "Well, thanks for a fun day."

"Yeah."

Oh, if only she could dream of marriage. Children. This man might just be worth it.

❧

Rayna stared at the Dallas skyline outside her office window.

"How could you?" Gabby's voice came from behind her.

She swung her chair around. "What?"

"I've waited all week long. All week long, and you haven't said a word. Don't you know I'm dying to know how your date went?"

Such drama tugged a grin out of her. "Actually, I had a great time." She frowned.

"Really?" Gabby perched in the burgundy wingback facing Rayna's mahogany desk. "Then why don't you look happy? Did he ask you out again?"

"Yes, but it didn't work out."

"So work around it."

"We have insurmountable differences." Rayna closed her eyes. "He wants a wife and kids."

"I'd nab him. Not many men are into that."

I'm not into that. I can't be.

"In the meantime, we've been summoned to Adam's office."

"Why?"

Her friend shrugged.

"We'd better go find out." Rayna slid her feet into the bronze-colored heels under her desk. Smoothing her coppery silk jacket and skirt, she followed Gabby to the office at the end of the hall.

Gabby tapped on the door, and Adam beckoned them inside. A man decked in a western suit, complete with white-stitched seams, sat in an art deco chair.

Behind his black desk, Adam's fake smile didn't cover the real scowl behind it. "Ah, here they are. Mr. Thornton, this is Gabrielle Curtis, our copywriter, and Rayna Landers, our art director. Two of our best execs. They'll make Clay Warren a star, even outside rodeo circles."

Rayna stifled a gasp.

Gabby's eyes widened.

She'd kill him. *Not really, Lord.* He'd said his sponsor wanted publicity and asked for her card. But she never dreamed he'd call after they'd decided to go their separate ways.

Adam's jaw clenched. "And as a result, every woman and girl will want their men and boys to wear what he's wearing."

"Nice to meet y'all." The man removed his hat. "I'm Clay's publicity manager. Call me Billy. Like Billy Bob Thornton, only my middle name ain't Bob. It's Joe. Anyway, we wanna put our Champion Bull Riding star and Cowboy Western Wear on the map. I want everyone to know who he is, what he's wearing, and where to get it. From the most rabid rodeo fan to the most disinterested, sophisticated debutante on Rodeo Drive."

The door opened behind them, and Rayna turned to see the man of her recent dreams.

Clay's hair was mussed. A dark smear marred his cheek, and matching grime soiled his clothing. Despite the grunge, her heart still sped.

"Sorry I'm late. Had a flat tire."

"I was wondering." Billy slapped Clay on the back. "Usually, ol' Clay here is early. The most reliable cowboy I know. And clean, too. Usually."

"What'd I miss?"

"This here's Adam, Gabrielle, and Rayna. They're our new advertising team. Meet the man of the hour himself, Clay Warren."

"Actually, I've met everyone except the pretty brunette." He wiped his hand down the side of his jeans and offered it to Gabby.

Out of character, her friend blushed. "You can call me Gabby."

Guess he has that effect on all females.

Adam glared.

"Nice to meet you, Gabby. Adam, good to see you again. And Rayna, of course." He nodded in her direction.

"What we need is some sort of slogan." Mr. Thornton spread his arms out as if describing the big fish that got away. "Something bigger than life, like Clay himself."

"Ten foot tall and bull proof." Rayna hadn't meant to utter the words aloud.

All eyes turned to her. Clay flashed a crooked grin that jolted her heart.

"You know, I like it." Mr. Thornton tapped his chin with his index finger. "Much ado's been made about Clay's height. Most bull riders are under six feet. Use that. Build a whole campaign around it. And make sure you keep this little lady on our team."

Great. Just great.

"Let's go to the conference room." Adam stood. "We can spread out and work more efficiently there."

"Gabby, show Mr. Thornton and Mr. Warren the way. Rayna and I will be there in a minute." Adam ushered the others out into the hall.

"Mind if I find a little boys' room and try to spruce up?" Clay held two grease-covered palms up.

"It's right around the corner." Gabby led the way.

Adam sighed as the door closed behind them. "Are you seeing him?"

"We went out once but learned we don't have much in common. Are you my father or my brother?" *I'm not a teenager.*

"I don't like him. Never liked those cocky types, daring enough to make moves on your little sister right under your nose. And now he's flirting with my. . .with Gabby."

My Gabby? "He didn't *make moves* on me, and he's not what you think. He's a Christian."

"He hired this firm to get closer to you." Adam rubbed the back of his neck.

"I don't know why he came here." Rayna shrugged, keeping

her tone even, despite the tremor in her soul.

Adam framed his hands in the air, outlining the imagined headline. "Weekend Warrior—Champion Bull Rider. We didn't even have to work for this account. I guess we should embrace what's landed in our laps."

ಶ

An hour.

One whole hour in the same room with Clay.

Rayna scanned the numerous notes sketching out the initial ad campaign littered across the long walnut conference table. If only Clay would go, maybe she could think straight.

Instead, he sat directly across from her.

"What's a weekend warrior?"

"There's your cowboys who travel with a certain rodeo all season." Clay cleared his throat. "Then there are your weekend warriors, the ones who, due to home, family, or business, don't travel far. They rodeo on weekends only, close to home. My dad won the Texas Circuit Finals and National Circuit Finals four years in a row." His tone had a humble awe to it.

Adam flipped through Clay's press release. "You've won the Fort Worth Stockyards Finals and the Horizon Series three times, and the CBR World title twice. Impressive."

Clay's posture changed, shoulders sagged. "Last year's injury kept me out of the gate for the world title. But I have a feeling—this year—it's gonna be my year."

"At the top of the standings for CBR World," Mr. Thornton reminded. "The top five riders in the Horizon Series are eligible to compete in the CBR Cinch Tour, a televised tour that airs on the Great American Country network. The Cinch finale determines the CBR World Champion."

"No wonder CWW decided to publicize you." Gabby sipped her coffee. "What is CBR?"

"Championship Bull Riding." Clay shifted in his chair, seeming uncomfortable with Billy's list of his accolades. "It's an organization that promotes pro bull riding. Friday nights at the Cowtown Coliseum are CBR sanctioned and part of the Horizon Series."

"So all the riders there are pro?" Rayna kept her gaze on her notes.

"It's an open rodeo. Local talent, just starting out, pro—it doesn't matter. You don't have to qualify. You just ride if you want to. A unique place where everybody gets a shot at their dream."

"We'll need tickets for your next rodeo." Adam closed his files.

"Done." Clay dug several tickets from his pocket and set them on the table. "Saturday night."

"Ten foot tall and bull proof. Brilliant." Mr. Thornton smacked Rayna on the back so hard her teeth rattled.

"But I didn't—"

"Brains and beauty." Clay winked at her from across the table.

Adam shot Clay a glare. "I've got a meeting. Gabby, I'll trust you to keep an eye on. . .things."

"It looks like Clay's in good hands." Mr. Thornton checked his watch. "I better get."

"Thanks Billy. I'll call you with the details." Clay pushed his chair back, massaging the back of his neck. "Could somebody direct me to the nearest coffeepot?"

"I'll get it." Gabby shot Rayna a grin.

"If you'll kindly tell me where it is, I can wait on myself."

"It's not a problem." Gabby scurried out.

Clay scrubbed a hand over his jaw. "How many commercials are we doing?"

Rayna stood and propped her hands on both hips. "What exactly are you up to?"

"Nothing. CWW was looking for an advertising firm. Thought persuading them to hire yours would be good for both our careers." He rounded the long table, stopping uncomfortably close to her.

"But. . ." *We decided not to see each other anymore.*

He shrugged. "You gave me your card, so I looked up your work on the Net. You made that NASCAR guy a household name last year. Seems this company is one of the best."

She pinched the dull ache at the bridge of her nose. "How did Adam get involved in this? We have several other creative directors."

"Now I didn't ask for him. Don't know how he got in the mix, but we're all adults. There's no reason we can't buck it up and work together. He should be happy." Clay splayed his hands, palms up. "I didn't get the girl."

She turned away, closing her eyes. "You're right. We're professionals."

"Did I get enough tickets? Got anyone else who might want to come?"

Mustering her resolve, she turned back to face him and scooped up the tickets.

"This is fine." She read the address. "The Fort Worth Stockyards? Sounds familiar. Is that at the fair?"

"It's a historical district, sort of an Old West town."

"I remember now. Originally part of the Chisholm Trail Cattle Drive."

"They have a cattle drive there twice a day. Cowtown Coliseum held the first indoor rodeo in 1918 and introduced bull riding in 1934."

"That actually sounds interesting." *Except for the bull riding part.* "A good place for a photo shoot. Could we shoot at a live rodeo there?"

"If you must." Clay shoved his hands in his pockets. "What do you have against the fair anyway? You liked the Peanut Festival."

"I like the fair. Just not the stench, the grease, or the music."

He laughed. "Let me guess. Your brother took you to see the pigs and other critters then tried to feed you?"

Rayna shivered. She could almost smell the livestock.

"Did you ride any rides?"

"No. Adam has motion sickness."

"Allow me to show you a good time at the fair." He took off his hat and held it to his chest. "Tell you what. I'll meet you at your place, say three o'clock, and we'll head to the fair and spend a few hours then on to the rodeo from there."

"But—"

"Relax. Two friends, two coworkers, enjoying the fair together. It's not a date. You can even ask the rest of the creative team to join us."

If only it could be a date. She must be insane. "Okay."

He winked. "See you tomorrow."

And the next day, and the next, and the next. The door shut behind him. She closed her eyes. Spending so much time with Clay? Pure pleasure—and torture.

❧

Clay pulled into the drive at the ranch house with his heart in his boots.

"How'd it go?" His best friend's wife perched on the arena fence while her student rode a sorrel mare. Hooves created dust clouds with each step.

"I'm officially a glorified male model, Lacie."

"It's not like you had much choice, and it's a brilliant move. You'll be a household name and this place will boom."

He groaned. "Son of four-time bull-riding champ sells himself out as a male model."

"Oh, it won't kill you. Think of how the hands won't be looking for jobs."

"Only reason I'm doing it." He hung his head. "But there's more. Remember that girl I told you 'bout?"

"The one you met at the fair? The ad exec, who doesn't want to get married?"

"Rayna. That's the one. I convinced Cowboy Western Wear to hire her firm for the campaign."

"You didn't."

"I even requested her on the project."

Lacie jumped from the fence. "What are you trying to do?" She propped both delicate hands on her hips.

What was it with women and that stance? "It seemed like a good idea at the time."

"Okay, so you're attracted to this girl."

"I could fall real easy. Feel myself teetering every time I look at her."

"But she doesn't want any of the things you do. Now why would you mess around and make it so you see her every day?"

Clay shrugged. It didn't make much sense. "'Cuz I want to see her every day?"

"And how do you think that'll improve the situation? Seeing the girl of your dreams every day, but she doesn't share your dreams."

"Maybe she'll fall for me, do a complete turnaround, and want three kids."

Lacie bit her lip. "Is there any undoing the advertising thing?"

"No. Billy finalized the deal with the owner this morning."

"Who's Billy?"

Clay groaned again. "The publicity agent CWW saddled me with."

She tried to suppress a grin.

"I saw that." He pointed at her. "I'm glad you find my discomfort so amusing."

"Did you warn Rayna?"

He kicked at a clod of dirt. Why didn't he think of that? She might have handled working with him better had she been forewarned. "Nope. Sprung it on her with my presence."

With an exaggerated sigh, she looked heavenward.

"She's the art director, so she'll have to supervise all the photo shoots. I even roped her into coming to the fair and the rodeo with me tomorrow night."

"Think you might grow on her?"

"I hope."

"Oh Clay, you have to want the same things. If you don't, life is. . ." Unshed tears flooded Lacie's eyes. "Very trying."

"Hey, what's wrong?"

"Nothing."

"You and Mel are okay, aren't you?"

"We're great." She swiped at the tears and looked past him. "My next student's here. Gotta get back to work."

ھ

Rayna stared at the galley proof the graphics designer had dreamed up. Billy had provided a picture of Clay, handsome and confident, astride her worst nightmare—a massive man-stomping bull. She couldn't focus on Gabby's copy either.

"You okay?" Gabby's voice came from the doorway.

How long had her friend been there? "Just kind of uncomfortable with the new campaign."

"I can imagine." Gabby set a cup of coffee on the desk. "Here. I haven't tasted it yet. Looks like you could use it more than me."

Rayna sipped the steaming liquid. Needed more creamer. "Thanks."

"What do you think of the copy?"

"Haven't gotten past the picture."

"He's definitely easy on the eyes." Gabby patted Rayna's shoulder. "But he's not as cute as Adam."

Rayna raised an eyebrow. Mission accomplished. "Clay talked me into going to the fair."

Gabby grinned. "You're going out with him again. I knew you two hit it off."

"It's not a date. He thinks I'll enjoy the fair if we stay away from the barns."

"Mm-hmm." Gabby crossed her arms over her chest.

"He invited the entire creative team and gave me tickets for everyone for the Saturday night rodeo at the Fort Worth Stockyards."

"I'll be at both places. But with my date."

"Adam? Awesome." And it was, except Rayna was stuck going to the fair. With Clay. Alone.

ھ

Rayna waited in her car as Clay pulled into the parking lot of her condo and stepped out of his truck. Cowboy to the bone. His pearl-studded black shirt and blue jeans revved her heart to double time.

Her most worn jeans, tennis shoes, and grape button-down blouse didn't compare. *If only I owned suitable clothing for the fair and the rodeo.* Did she really just think that?

With a wink, he sauntered over to lean in the window. "Are you the only taker?"

I will not fall for the cowboy. I will not fall for the cowboy.

Maintain professional aloofness. "Guess so." *Don't look at him.* "Actually, Gabby and Adam will be there, but they're going together. I'll drive my car."

"Nonsense. No need in you dealing with this traffic. Ride with me."

Surely he could hear her pounding heart. *Come up with a great excuse.* Why did he always create cobwebs in her cowboy-dazed brain? "Okay, but we're just riding together. This is not—"

"A date. I know." He opened the door for her and flashed a knee-jolting grin.

four

The good thing about her height, Rayna had no trouble getting out of Clay's way-too-high four-wheel drive.

"I was coming to help."

"I managed."

They began the long trek across miles of asphalt to the admission gate.

He slowed his swagger to match her stride. "Have you always lived in Texas?"

"Born and raised."

"How can you live here your whole life and never go to a rodeo?"

"Daddy always said they were silly, but he used to take me to a dude ranch as a kid." *Until I had an asthma attack there.*

"But you're an adult now. You've lived on your own awhile."

"I guess they never interested me." *Might as well tell him his livelihood bores me brainless.* "Sorry."

The gulf between them stretched wider.

Big Tex didn't say anything as they entered the gate, and Rayna gazed up at the huge statue, shielding her eyes from the sun. "Why isn't he talking tonight?"

"He only talks on the hour. We missed it." Clay turned away from the stockyards, toward the neon lights and thumping music. "What kind of music do you like?"

"Symphony."

"Are you sure you were born in Texas?"

She laughed. "Daddy wanted us to be cultured. He took us to a lot of art galleries, symphonies, museums, and plays."

"Not the fair or Six Flags?"

"A few times when we were little."

"Do you like roller coasters?"

"I love them."

"There's that risk taker."

For the next hour, Rayna screamed, laughed, and lost her stomach. After the roller coaster, the Tornado shot them high in the sky and twirled until she thought she'd lose her lunch. The Tilt-A-Whirl flung her soundly against Clay's chest, where he held her so tight, she could feel his heartbeat.

The ride stopped. Regretful and dizzy, she pushed away from him and clambered out of the cozy cocoon.

He steadied her. "I hate to break up the party, but the rodeo starts soon."

"That's okay." Rayna clutched her stomach. "I've had enough. But it was so much fun. I haven't done that in years."

"Maybe we could go to Six Flags sometime, too. You okay?"

"Standing." She wobbled. "Barely, that is."

He laughed. "Let's get something to eat."

"Is there anything without grease?"

" 'Fraid not." He surveyed the line of booths. "Let's see. You like chicken, don't you?"

"Grilled."

"It's not exactly grilled, but I bet you'll love the chicken on a stick."

"Sounds interesting."

Clay took her hand.

Warmth spread over her as they maneuvered through the press of the crowd. Numerous concession stands lined the area with the heavy essence of deep-fried batter.

He pointed to a bench. "Wait over there. No sense in you standing in line, too."

Couldn't she trail behind him and keep holding his hand? With a nod, she took a seat. Rayna tried to people-watch but couldn't keep her eyes off Clay. Every time he looked as if he might turn in her direction, her gaze darted away. Needing a distraction, she pulled her phone out of her pocket. Five texts from Gabby: Where r u?

She punched in Food Court and looked up as the vendor handed Clay their food. Rayna pretended extreme interest in the passing crowd.

"Here you go." He offered a grease-splotched, white-paper-wrapped item and a large lemonade.

She stifled a wince.

A grin twitched Clay's lips. "Try it. If you don't like it, you can munch on unbuttered popcorn or something, or I'll find a salad for you to graze on when we head home. But just try it."

Rayna unrolled the paper to find greasy fried coating with a shish kebab stuck through it. She started to pull the breading away, but he grabbed her hand.

"One bite."

Closing her eyes, she sank her teeth into the deep-fried chicken, onion, and the unexpected tang of dill pickle bathed in grease. "I can feel my arteries clogging, but it's so worth it."

"Good, huh? My favorite. I usually buy several, take them home and freeze them."

Gabby and Adam rounded a concession stand booth, her hand firmly engulfed in his. Her eyes lit up. "Hey, y'all made it."

"We've been here awhile." Clay tipped his hat. "Riding rides."

"We toured all the stockyards." Adam pulled Gabby to his side as if he thought Clay might try to steal her away.

Rayna cleared her throat. "I'm here for research."

"Researching the roller coasters?" Clay winked.

"That was your idea."

"Hey Adam, when we get to the rodeo, can we talk?" Clay asked.

Adam swallowed. "Sure."

"I'll meet you in the lobby near the main entrance."

"Let's get something to eat before we go." Gabby tugged Adam toward the concession stands.

"See you there." Rayna waved. What did Clay want to talk to Adam about?

Clay rolled their trash into a wad and sank it in the garbage can like a pro basketball player. "Hey, wanna ride a bull?"

The hair along the back of her neck stood on end. "You're kidding, right?"

"No." He motioned, and she followed his gaze. "A mechanical bull."

The rawhide-draped dummy moved slowly then spun, and the little boy astride tumbled off, giggling all the way to the cushioned mat. Then the bull ducked its head and prodded the child with a fake horn.

"Come on. It'll be fun. I'll go first."

Clay paid for both rides and mounted the fake bull.

"Hey, that's Clay Warren!" a heavyset woman shouted.

Soon a massive crowd circled the area.

Again, the bull started moving slowly but picked up speed in seconds. Rocking, spinning, and bucking, it never came anywhere near throwing Clay. To applause, he dismounted with ease and returned to her side.

"Okay, your turn."

"I don't think so."

"Where's that risk taker with barbecue sauce on her chin? Go on." He nudged her toward the dummy and the crowd clapped louder.

Rayna climbed aboard. The attendee showed her where to hold and insisted she keep one hand in the air. As soon as the mechanical ride began, she grabbed on with both hands. Despite her good grip, one jerky whirl later, she landed in a heap on the mat.

Dizzy and stomach twisting, she laughed along with the crowd as Clay applauded and whistled. The bull concentrated on butting her backside until she managed to scramble out of its range.

"You sure were a good sport."

"It looked easy. Especially with you up there, like you could stay on forever."

"I've had a little practice."

She and Clay stayed to watch a few more hapless souls meet the same fate as Rayna then headed toward the truck.

The seventy-two-foot cowboy waved as they exited.

"See you next year, Big Tex." Clay tipped his hat.

&

Cowtown Coliseum's lobby bustled with folks. Concession lines snaked through the corral there.

Clay took off his hat and clutched it against his thudding heart. Win over the brother, win over the girl? Tension emanated from Adam.

Gabby and Rayna had gone to the restroom while a bull waited for Clay. Part of him wished he could sit in the stands with her and watch instead. Even though he'd spent the afternoon with her, he longed for more.

"What did you want to talk about?" Adam's tone was all business.

"Listen, if we're gonna work together, we need to call a truce. Seems you and me, we got off on the wrong boot."

"A novel way to put it."

"I'm sorry for liking your sister, but Rayna and I aren't seeing each other."

"You just ride roller coasters together?" Adam raised an eyebrow.

"Okay, I'm interested in her. I admit it." Clay jammed his hat back on. "But she's not. So are we okay?"

"As long as you don't mess with my sister."

"I'm not the type of guy who *messes* with women. I'm not looking for a bed partner." Clay grinned. "Not until after the wedding anyway, and I want a lifetime partner. I respect women and my God who created them. Look, are you a Christian?"

Adam's jaw clenched. "Yes."

"We're both trying to find the girl of our dreams who loves Jesus. Can we get past this tension?"

"I'm not tense." Adam frowned, stiff as a two-by-eight.

"I made a bad first impression, and now you think I'm after everything female. Gabby is a lovely girl, but I'm not interested in her. Even if I were, she only has eyes for you. Look at her." Clay motioned to the two returning women. "Who's she staring at?"

"Me." A huge smile stole over Adam's face.

"If Rayna comes around to my way of thinking about us, I vow to do my best not to hurt her." Clay offered his hand. "Either way, can we be friends?"

~

Rayna relaxed as the two men shook hands. Adam's rock-hard features softened as she and Gabby neared.

"They look like they're getting along better. You'll sit with us, won't you?" Gabby sounded sincere.

Third wheel. No, thank you.

Adam reached for Gabby's hand. "Clay wants to show Rayna a good place to take pictures. We'd better find seats."

"See you Monday." Thankful for the rescue, Rayna hurried to keep up with Clay's swagger.

"What were you and Adam talking about?"

"We made peace." Clay threaded his fingers through hers and led her toward the arena. "I assured him I'm not some wolf out to conquer every woman I see."

As they stepped inside the arena, the stench of manure hit her full force. However, the music wasn't quite as annoying. Maybe it was the company. Corrals lined both ends of the arena. Clay led her down a narrow path with a wall on her left and the iron fence surrounding the arena on her right. An enormous tractor sat in the middle of the freshly plowed dirt.

Clay turned and climbed a few steps into the stands. "My friends have box seats over here." Folding chairs lined the boxes with walls around three sides. Behind the boxes, stationary metal chairs with folding seats lined the stands.

A pretty blond waved from a box. A man exemplifying cowboy stood by her side—long camel duster over chaps and pearl-studded shirt, complete with boots and the mandatory hat.

"This is my newly hired art director for the ad campaign." Clay raked dark curls away from his face and jammed his hat on. "Rayna, meet my best friend in the whole world, Mel Gentry, and his wife, Lacie."

She looked like a country-and-western star, complete with

big hair and rhinestone-dripping denim. Yet the look suited her petite frame. When Rayna offered her hand, Lacie greeted her with a warm embrace instead. Her husband followed suit with a brotherly bear hug.

"Almost time to start. Y'all better git." Lacie kissed her husband then wagged a red fingernail in his face. "Now, you be careful."

"Lacie, you watch out for her." Clay's eyes sparkled. "I'm trusting you to keep the cowboys at bay. Rayna's here to work."

As if any other cowboy's appeal could come anywhere near Clay's.

Rayna cleared her throat. "I brought my camera. Thought I might get a few shots."

He pointed to the maze of corrals lining the left end of the arena. "That's where most of the action is." He finally let go of her hand and tipped his hat. "See you later."

Her heart continued to rattle in her chest as he loped away.

"Tell me about yourself." Lacie sat and patted the seat beside her. "What does an art director do?"

Rayna settled on the unyielding aluminum. "I handle the graphics and layouts for print ads, supervise video and photo shoots, and snap a few pictures myself. How about you?"

"During the week, Mel and I work the ranch with Clay. Weekends, we do this."

"What do you do at the ranch?"

"Mel works the cattle. I teach kids to ride." A wistful smile lit Lacie's blue eyes.

"Do you and Mel have children?"

The smile tilted downward. "I've always put it off—afraid something might happen to Mel, and I'd end up alone—with a baby to raise."

"Is he ill?"

"No. That man's as strong as a Clydesdale."

"Then what could happen?" Rayna figured they were only in their mid to late twenties.

The music stopped.

"Ladies and Gentlemen, welcome to the Stockyard's Championship Rodeo," the announcer's voice boomed.

Rayna jumped.

The tractor roared to life then lumbered to the end of the arena where Clay and Mel had disappeared in a mass of Stetson-clad heads. A gate opened and the tractor exited.

"God Bless the USA" began playing over the speakers, and a girl dressed in blue sequins holding an American flag rode into the arena on a white horse. Slowly, she rounded the arena until the song built to a climax, and the horse ran faster and faster. By the time the horse and rider exited, Rayna was misty-eyed. Her vision blurred even more as the announcer prayed.

He introduced a dark-haired cowgirl who walked to the middle of the arena and sang "The Star Spangled Banner."

As the closing notes faded away and the singer exited, the announcer gave a short history of Cowtown Coliseum and introduced three clowns. Loud, thumping music began playing. A rock song at a rodeo?

"For our first event of the evening: bull riding."

"My least favorite event." Lacie clenched her teeth and pointed to their left. "Those are the bucking chutes."

Something slammed against metal. Rayna jumped. Bulls rammed into tiny pens. Cowboys clustered around one chute as a rider stood on the fence, hovering over the bull. Rayna shivered.

"Those are the roping chutes." Lacie pointed to their right where calves waited in corrals.

"What do they do with the calves?"

"Calf roping—my second least favorite event." Lacie sighed. "The guys ride horses. When they turn the calves loose, the guys rope them. Then they throw them down and tie three of their legs together."

Rayna winced. "Do Clay and Mel do that?"

Blond waves danced with an emphatic shake of Lacie's head. "They used to, but I complained about the inhumanity of it until they quit."

"Good. Doesn't sound like something I'll enjoy watching."

"Mel and Clay are in the second round. Let's go get something to wet our whistles, and I'll introduce you around."

Going against the flow of traffic, they picked their way through the crowd then maneuvered to the short line at the concession booth. A group of women gathered to one side.

"None of the girls like the calf roping. We usually hang out in the lobby till it's over. I'll introduce you, and you can visit while I get our drinks. What do you want?"

"Bottled water."

"You sure? The sweet tea's really good."

"Maybe next time." What was she saying? There wouldn't be a next time. Surely one rodeo would give her all the experience she needed for the campaign.

Lacie stopped at the fringe of the gathering of women. "Girls, this is Rayna. Make her feel welcome."

"Clay's girl?" A tall woman raised one brow.

Rayna didn't want to admit how much she liked the sound of it.

"I'll leave you to tackle that one." Lacie turned away.

"No. I'm an advertising executive, hired by Mr. Warren's publicist. I'm here to work."

Raising her camera for all to see, Rayna caught the glare of pure dislike from a raven-haired woman. Pouty lips curled into a forced smile like a mask slipping into place. The woman sashayed over with an exaggerated twist of her hips and extended her hand. "I'm Natalie." Her fuchsia nails dug into Rayna's palm. "This is Christy, Gloria. . ."

As the list went on, Rayna pulled her hand away. Fire swept through her veins. She knew exactly what Natalie's problem was.

"Ready?" Lacie handed Rayna her water. "Sounds like the first round of bulls and calf roping's over."

"Nice meeting y'all." Rayna turned toward her new friend. Numerous "see you laters" followed but none offered by Natalie.

Again, they went against the flow of traffic back to their box seats. "Clay will be riding soon, and this'll be a great spot for pictures."

"What's with Natalie?"

"She's after Clay." Lacie smirked.

"I thought it was something like that." She swallowed hard. "Is he interested?"

"No way. She's tried to sink her talons into him for years." Lacie held both hands up like claws. "Her folks live next door to his. She's been after him since high school, probably even before that."

"Why hasn't he taken the bait?"

"First of all, she's not a Christian and has no interest in becoming one. Secondly, she's rather promiscuous."

A gate at the side of the arena opened and numerous children ran to the center, where the three clowns joined them. "What's going on?"

Lacie giggled. "Now this is my favorite. The calf scramble. They tie a ribbon to its tail and turn it loose. The kids have to try to get the ribbon."

A chute opened to their right and a calf ran into the arena. The mass of kids chased after it. The calf made loops and spins, staying out of range. Just as it appeared the scramble might last all night, one boy made his move and held up the ribbon. The exit gate at the left of the arena opened, and the calf escaped.

"Looks like we've got a winner. You can get your prize in the lobby."

The children cleared the arena.

"Ladies and Gentlemen, and now for a real treat—team roping."

"Oh great." Lacie slapped her knee.

To their right, cows with horns waited in gated corrals. "Do Clay and Mel do this?"

"I've tried to dissuade them, but they insist it doesn't hurt the steers."

Cowboys, including Clay and Mel, lined up to the left of the chutes.

"They don't throw those things down, do they?"

"No. Clay's the header and Mel's the heeler."

"The what?"

"Clay ropes the horns and Mel ropes the hind feet." Patience resonated in Lacie's tone.

"Then what?"

"They stretch the poor critter out between them until it can't go anywhere. Trust me. It's better than roping a calf and wrestling it to the ground."

Rayna cringed. "Is there anything happening tonight that I might want to watch?"

"I like the barrel racing. The broncs are okay. They don't make me too nervous, but I hate the bulls." Lacie trembled.

Rayna stiffened.

Though she felt sorry for the steers, the precision with which the two cowboys lassoed horns and heels fascinated her. Dust flew as hoofbeats narrowed in on the hapless creatures.

"How do they decide who wins?"

"Each team gets five- and ten-second penalties if they only get one heel or break the barrier and stuff like that. Whoever gets the fastest time wins."

"What's the barrier?"

"It's complicated, but it's sort of like a head start for the steer. If they cross the laser line too soon, they get penalized." Lacie let out a whoop. "Here's Mel and Clay."

Rayna raised her camera, snapped numerous shots, and instinctively knew several were perfect. Though she concentrated mainly on Clay, since it was a team event, she took some of Mel as well.

"Clay Warren and Mel Gentry handily win the competition," the announcer boomed. "These two rough riders set the bar high."

Rayna and Lacie jumped to their feet to applaud. What was she doing? Clapping because two men picked on a cow?

Throughout the evening, the barrel clown joked back and forth with the announcer, lightening some intense moments.

Loud music—everything from country to rock—played during each event. Between events the sparkling girl on the white horse rode around the arena with various flags bearing logos of the rodeo's sponsors.

For the sheep scramble, kids once again invaded the arena. A gate from the roping chutes opened and the sheep ran straight to the exit gate on the other end, stood, and waited for it to open. A boy easily grabbed the ribbon from the woolly back.

"That was one cooperative sheep," the announcer chuckled. "Next up, barrel racing."

Rayna enjoyed the event, even when Natalie, decked out in hot pink and sequins, raced her horse around the arena. She did well but didn't win. A few minutes later, Rayna spotted her. With her hands balled into fists, she stomped toward the lobby.

Rayna stifled a grin.

"Ladies and Gentlemen, hold on to your hats. It's time for bareback bronc riding. First up, two-time CBR World Champ, Claaaaay Warrrrrrren."

The crowd erupted in whistles and cheers.

A gate flew open and a horse careened into the arena bucking and twisting. On its back, Clay hung on for dear life.

"What's it doing?" Rayna forced herself to aim the camera.

"Trying to buck him off."

"But why?"

"They're bred to buck."

"But what if he falls?" The horse jolted Clay, and Rayna wanted to hide her eyes.

"That's the point. To stay on."

"Hold on, Clay!" she yelled. "Use both hands."

The buzzer sounded as Lacie giggled.

"What?"

Lacie tried to stifle a smile. "It's against the rules to hang on with both hands."

Clay leaped from the back of the horse and sauntered out of the arena unfazed.

"That was a really good ride." Lacie put her thumb and finger between her lips and delivered an earsplitting whistle worthy of any man.

"A fine ride and a fine score of eighty-six by Claaaayyy Warrennnnn."

Several horses managed to buck other riders off before the buzzer sounded. However, each walked away. Even when they fell, her heart didn't pound the way it had when her cowboy was in jeopardy.

My cowboy?

"How do they decide who wins?"

"They have to stay on for eight seconds, without flopping around. They get deductions if they touch the bronc with their free hand, and added points the more the bronc bucks and twists. Things like that. Right now Clay's still in the lead." Lacie pointed to the chute. "Oh, here's Mel."

Though nothing like during Clay's ride, Rayna's concern intensified until Mel's eight seconds ended. As he dismounted, Lacie jumped to her feet to cheer her husband on.

Rayna followed suit. "Was that good?"

Lacie pointed to the scoreboard. "He beat Clay's score."

"Does that bother them? I mean, when they beat each other?"

"No, they're just happy for each other. Okay, it's bull-riding time. Cross all your fingers and toes."

Bulls crammed in chutes, butting and hurling themselves into the gates. Clay planned to ride one of those things? Was he insane?

"And now, Ladies and Gentlemen, for the final event of the evening. It's time to separate the men from the boys. Bulllll ridddinnng." The announcer's voice echoed through the coliseum. "And first up, once again, two-time CBR World Champ, Clayyyyy Warrrrennnnn."

Rayna got a glimpse of Clay hovering above a bull in one of the chutes. She closed her eyes.

"Now, the rules are a lot like the broncs." Lacie leaned forward. "The more the bull jumps, spins, and bucks, the more points each rider gets. They get points for style, kinda like if they can stay in rhythm with the bull and not flop around. Again, their free hand can't touch the bull, and they have to stay on for eight seconds."

Lacie pointed across the arena. "That clown over there—he's a bullfighter. He'll help the cowboy get out of the arena in one piece. Sometimes, they cheer the bull on so the rider gets more points. And over there, the barrel clown distracts the bull. He can hide in his barrel, if needed, until the pick-up man"—she pointed to a cowboy on horseback—"helps the bull rider to safety or gets the bull out of the arena. They're the heroes of the rodeo."

Clay burst forth from the gate astride a massive ivory beast. The frenzied crowd cheered and chanted. Rayna focused enough to snap several shots. The bull kicked its heels so high she thought it would surely topple over onto its back and crush Clay. His leather chaps flapped with each jolt. A pain stabbed her chest, constricting her breathing. If not for the noise, she could have sworn she was wheezing.

"Are you all right?" Lacie's voice came from far away. Her blue eyes reflected worry. "Rayna, what's wrong?"

She couldn't answer, struggling for breath as the bull twisted then threw its head back. If Clay slid forward the tiniest bit, he'd be gored.

five

Lacie grasped Rayna's arm.

Rayna couldn't move, transfixed by the scene but no longer capable of capturing any of it on film.

A buzzer sounded. Clay jumped from the bull's back and the enormous creature charged. The bullfighter distracted the beast while Clay climbed the fence.

Rayna dug her inhaler from her purse and took two puffs.

"Calm down, hon. Take deep breaths."

The pain in her chest eased, and her airflow increased.

"You okay?"

She nodded, trying to make light of the situation. "Probably something in the air triggered an attack."

"Scared me. You sure you're okay?"

"Fine. Could you not tell Clay? He doesn't know about my asthma. It's kind of embarrassing."

"There's nothing to be embarrassed about." Lacie patted her shoulder.

"He'll think I can't handle this job."

"Whatever you think, hon."

"Maybe I got some good pictures anyway." She mustered up a weak smile.

❧

What had happened back there? She hadn't had an attack in months. In fact, she'd almost taken her inhaler out of her purse.

Rayna prayed Clay couldn't tell how unnerved she was. His dusty chaps swished with each step as they walked through the cowboy-crowded rear exit. True to her word, Lacie hadn't told on her. Cool night air hit her in the face. Rayna gulped deep breaths.

"You okay?"

"Fresh air is nice."

"I hope you're not claustrophobic."

Only when bulls are around.

He gestured to the back of Old West buildings next to the coliseum. "These are original. I'd love to give you a tour someday. There's the Cowboy Hall of Fame, Cowboy Museum, even an art gallery. Probably not your kind of museum or gallery, but come spring, we could ride the train." Clay tucked her hand in his elbow.

A slow train ride? With Clay? No thanks.

He opened the truck door for her then hurried around and started the engine. "What'd you think of your first rodeo?"

"It was different than anything I've ever experienced." Slight understatement.

"Did you enjoy it?"

"Parts of it."

"What parts?"

"I liked the barrel race."

"Nothing that involved me, huh?" He sounded hurt.

"The steer roping was interesting, but those poor cows."

Clay laughed as he merged into the traffic.

"What?"

"A steer is a neutered bull."

"Oh." At least the darkness hid her blush. "Anyway, you're very good at what you do."

"But it didn't do it for you."

"The whole thing seemed dangerous." Another understatement.

"It can be. But we wear gear." He pounded his chest gorilla style. "I had on a vest stronger than steel to protect against internal injuries."

"What about a helmet?"

"I tried it a few times, but it threw my balance and vision off."

"Have you ever been seriously hurt?"

"I missed the Cinch finale last year with a broken collarbone." Clay massaged his shoulder as if it still hurt.

"I'm not even going to ask how it happened."

"Actually, it was my own fault. I dismounted wrong. But now, my dad, he's the king of bull-riding injuries."

"Does your dad still rodeo?" Shock echoed in her tone. Did lack of common sense run in the family?

"Not anymore. He retired from the circuit when I was a teenager. After his last surgery. Torn rotator cuff."

"What's a rotator cuff?"

"It's in your shoulder." He turned into the parking lot of her condo, found a space, and walked around to her side.

Rayna accepted the hand he offered and hopped down from the truck. "How many surgeries has he had?"

"I've lost count. Fifteen, maybe sixteen."

She pushed down the unknown shadows that threatened to invade her soul and concentrated on the moon instead— full and marshmallow-soft tonight.

"What in the world made you want to follow in his footsteps?" She slid her hands into her pockets.

"I guess it's in my blood. And then I found the dude ranch. Fell in love with it and knew that's what I wanted." Clay's eyes sparkled in the moonlight. "To allow kids who didn't have the advantage of growing up on a farm like I did to learn to ride horses. To provide city folk a chance to get away from it all and experience the beauty of the country."

Growing up on a farm an advantage? He made it sound worth envying.

"What does the rodeo have to do with that? It takes you away from the place you love."

"Yes, but it helps pay for the ranch."

"But aren't you afraid you'll get hurt?"

He shrugged. "I've spent hours watching tapes with my dad. Hours and hours of him and every other cowboy in the world. We analyze every time one of them falls and figure out what went wrong. Then I do my best to avoid the same mistakes. Last year's injury was the first I ever had."

But probably not his last. She stopped outside her door. "Thanks for taking me tonight. Guess I'll see you Monday."

"Good night then." He tipped his hat in true cowboy fashion then turned away.

Rayna stepped inside, turned the light on, and leaned against the door. Why had the rodeo affected her that way? She was used to Clay stealing her oxygen, but her reaction hadn't been about Clay.

If the sight of a bull in action literally took her breath away, how would she build a campaign around Clay?

With trembling fingers, she dialed the number.

He answered on the second ring. "Hello?"

"Daddy, anxiety can cause an asthma attack, right?"

"Are you okay, Rayna?" Concern echoed in his voice.

"I'm fine, but I went to a rodeo tonight." She perched on the arm of the sofa.

Her father gasped. "And you had an attack. Maybe it was something in the air or dust."

"I don't think so. I had the attack during the bull riding. That thing was so big and lethal looking. It made me really nervous, and the next thing I knew, I couldn't breathe."

"I see." His tone changed to clinical analyst. "How about not going again? That way you wouldn't be nervous."

"I'd love to never go again." She closed her eyes. "But I'm working on an ad campaign for a bull rider. My job requires me to hang out at the rodeo for a while."

"I see. In that case, make an appointment with your doctor. He may increase your dosage. In the meantime, use your inhaler before you go, and keep it in reach while you're there."

"Is she all right?" A woman's voice in the background.

A lump formed in Rayna's throat. Oops. Once again, she'd interrupted his evening. "I'm going to bed. Thanks, Daddy."

&

Only a few red and gold leaves clung to late-October branches. During the ride to Clay's ranch, Rayna had to put up with Kendra—the official photographer for the project— cracking cowboy jokes all the way. But at least Adam and Gabby had gotten to drive there together.

They followed Adam down a long drive and parked near an outdoor arena. Though it wasn't a real rodeo, the daylong photo shoot required a real bull. Rayna cringed at the large chocolate-colored monster.

Several cowboys on horseback stirred the outdoor arena into a dust bowl.

Maybe the dust at the rodeo had triggered her attack. Though there hadn't been as much in the indoor arena.

"Couldn't we do this at an indoor arena?" Kendra scrunched her nose.

"It was Billy's idea." Rayna's gaze riveted on the massive hump on the back of the bull's neck and the set of horns. She shivered.

Clay waved from his perch on the arena fence.

"Okay, this guy looks good enough," Kendra whispered. "I might date him myself, in spite of the cowboy thing."

"Trust me." Rayna stifled a sigh. "He's not your type."

Kendra flashed a smug it's-all-about-me smile. "We'll see."

The arena was quite impressive with an iron railing and a chute at each end. There was even a narrow row of bleacher-style seating.

As the shoot began, Rayna huddled behind the stands, calling out occasional directions as Kendra's flash flickered. Clay rode astride the massive monster, flung about like a flag. She flinched, hid her face with both hands, then peeked through her fingers.

Adam frowned. "You okay?"

"I really don't like bulls."

"I could put another art director on the project."

"No way. If he wins the world title again, this will be the biggest campaign we've ever landed. I'm fine."

"And stubborn," Adam muttered as he strode to the fence and climbed to the second rung to watch.

As ride after ride stretched into the afternoon, Clay never fell, and each time he dismounted, two bullfighters deterred the beast. All three men stayed safe.

After a while, Rayna came out of hiding. She stood near

the stands, arms crossed over her chest, nails digging into her forearms, praying.

He really was good at this. Actually, quite amazing. He hadn't been bucked off. Not once.

And no crushing weight had settled on her lungs either.

"Rayna, what do you think?" Adam called.

"About?"

"Do we have enough footage? I think our star is tired."

"And probably a bit sore." Kendra winced. "We definitely don't want to damage the handsome merchandise."

"Oh yes. That's a wrap," Rayna shouted. "Great job everyone."

Clay leaned on the rail fence to catch his breath.

"Ooh, wait." Kendra positioned her lens. "That's a good shot. Hold still. Come on. Relax. Stop frowning."

"Sorry. This isn't my thing."

"Think about something that makes you happy."

His gaze settled on Rayna, and a slow grin lifted one corner of his mouth.

"That's better." Kendra squatted and turned the camera sideways. "Must be thinking about your ranch."

"Something like that."

"Okay, now take your shirt off." Kendra adjusted her lens once more.

Clay tensed. "No."

"Oh, come on," Kendra purred. "The ladies will love it. They'll want their men to wear CWW jeans and no shirt just like that hunky Clay Warren."

"I'm no hunk."

If you say so. Rayna's face warmed even though she wouldn't mind seeing him shirtless.

Kendra repositioned her camera. "Just humor me."

"No, that's where I draw the line. This photo shoot is officially over." He ambled over to Rayna, effectively dismissing Kendra. "You headed back to the office?"

She checked her watch. "No. It's past quitting time."

"How about horseback riding and a hot dog roast?"

Alone with him? No way. But she'd love to ride. She turned to the others. "Good idea. How about it, guys?"

"Can't. I've got plans." Kendra didn't even try to hide her irritation and headed for her car.

Rayna's heart sank. What if everyone said no?

"Sounds like fun." Gabby elbowed Adam. "Want to stay?"

"Sure."

A relieved sigh escaped Rayna.

"Don't tell me you're afraid of me," Clay whispered.

As his breath stirred the hair at her ear, she shivered. *You terrify every intricately firing neuron of my brain.*

"Mind if I take Gabby out to the horse barn?" Adam tucked Gabby's hand inside his elbow.

"'Course not. Rayna can go in and meet the folks." Clay pressed a hand to the small of her back.

"No" wobbled on the tip of her tongue, but Gabby seemed pleased at the prospect of being alone with Adam. Keeping her mouth shut, Rayna stuffed her hands in her pockets.

"I thought the lovebirds could use some alone time."

"I hope it works out for them." Warmth swept through her as he started toward the house then slowed his stride to match hers. "Gabby's had a rough time this year, and she seems happy for a change."

"How long have they worked together?"

"We've all worked together five years."

"It's weird how you can have someone right under your nose for months, sometimes years, and suddenly notice them—in a romantic way—I mean."

Could he be talking about Natalie?

"It's not much farther now."

The woods widened into a clearing. White-rail fences everywhere, and in the middle of it all, a large rustic lodge.

"This is yours?"

"Yep. We've only got one family right now. Weather's been kind of chilly for riding, but with this nice warm front, today's perfect. Want to ride Buttercream before we eat?"

"Oh yes."

"Just let me get cleaned up. I smell like a bull, and I'm covered in dust."

She swallowed hard. But oh, it looked good on him.

A woman with faded auburn hair and a tall man swayed slowly on the porch swing.

"Hello, I'm Clay's mama, Durlene." A smattering of freckles covered her nose. Her lavender and white western shirt matched her cowgirl boots. "And this here's his daddy, Ty."

"I'm Rayna Landers."

The man—also clad in western clothing—met them on the steps with a slight limp. His thick, wavy silver hair contrasted with his still-black eyebrows. "Are you the girl who's been keeping our boy so busy?"

Clay's coloring definitely came from his dad. And his boldness.

"Rayna's my art director for the ad campaign."

"Sure that's all there is to it?"

Ty's wink warmed Rayna's face as she stepped up onto the porch.

" 'Fraid so. A few more of the crew will be here shortly. Can y'all keep Rayna occupied while I spruce up?"

"Please do that." Durlene pinched her nose.

Clay kissed his mom's cheek and disappeared inside.

The ranch boasted steak house décor, complete with spotted rawhide draping the windows and horseshoes gracing the cedar-plank walls.

"Let's go in the great room."

Pictures of bronc and bull riders lined the hallway.

Rayna stopped beside a faded photo. Though the bull turned her blood cold, she concentrated on the rider. It looked like Clay, yet the quality of the picture and clothing style suggested it was too old.

"This is you, isn't it?" She turned to Ty.

"Yep. Back in my day. The year Clay was born."

"Who are the others?"

"Friends, legends, heroes. This here's Lefty Shelton. He

was a real good friend." Ty took off his hat and clasped it against his heart. "Just took a wrong turn."

Something about the cowboy in the photo seemed familiar to Rayna. A chill crept up her spine.

"Here's the night Clay won his first world title."

The picture showed Clay tilting precariously forward while astride a colossal beast, its heels kicked high in the air. Clay's expression radiated pure joy. She shivered.

"And here's the second one. We'll have to move everything over and get another shot in here. Three-time CBR World Champion." Anticipation and pride echoed in Ty's voice. He ushered her to the great room.

"Do you all live here?"

"Clay has a suite on the second floor. Our house sits just a piece down the road, maybe three miles." Durlene plumped pillows on the navy plaid couch before sitting down. "But we both work here. I teach adult horseback riding and keep up with the books. Ty breaks horses."

"Do you ever get thrown?"

A deep chuckle came from the doorway. "I've scraped Dad off the arena floor a few times."

Clay had changed clothes. His damp hair curled even more.

A knock sounded at the door.

"That's probably Adam and Gabby." Clay ushered her down the hall. "Let's get some riding in before it gets dark."

❧

Clay tried not to grin as Rayna slid down Buttercream's side.

"Here." He linked his fingers together like his dad used to do when Clay was little.

"I'd rather use a mounting block. I might hurt your hands."

"No way. You don't weigh anything."

She placed her tennis-shoe-clad foot into his makeshift stirrup and swung her leg over the horse. He put his shoulder under her thigh and gave her a much-needed boost. A little bit of wallowing and she was in the saddle.

"That was the picture of grace." Her face almost matched

her hair. "I haven't done this since I was a kid."

His bay stood patiently while he tied their supper-filled saddlebag on her side. "Just like riding a bike. It'll come back."

He was right. Ten minutes down the wooded path and she looked like she'd been born in the saddle.

She scanned the woods. "I thought we'd have caught up with Gabby and Adam by now."

"I think they wanted to get lost."

"Adam said you're going somewhere next week?"

"I'll be in Colorado for the Cinch finale."

"The one that determines the world championship."

"That's the one."

"I hope you stay safe."

"Me, too."

"This place is beautiful."

"Let's stop here." He helped her dismount, a bit more tactfully, at his favorite spot he'd wanted to share with her. To the right, a rocky meadow; to the left, woods. Behind them, a majestic mountain.

"This is where I want to build my cabin with the woman I love."

She trembled.

"You cold?"

"A little."

"Sun'll be setting soon." He could give her his blue-jean jacket. Instead, he stepped close and tilted her chin up with tender fingers then lowered his lips toward hers. Her russet eyelashes fluttered closed.

six

Thundering hoofbeats approached. Despite quivery legs, Rayna backed away from Clay.

Mel rode into the clearing on a big black horse.

"Doggone it, Mel. We need to work on your timing."

More hoofbeats approached, and Lacie's coppery horse stopped beside Mel's.

"Clay Warren, what are you up to? Taking that little girl out in the woods." Lacie winked.

Maybe winking was a rodeo thing. The usual heat moved over Rayna's face. Maybe it was a rodeo thing to be bold.

"Hush, Lacie, you're embarrassing Rayna. And besides, you know I'm a perfect gentleman. I answer to Jesus. Just showing off my favorite spot."

"And we interrupted." Mel swung down from his horse with ease. "But we've got big news. Lacie's pregnant."

Lacie swung off her horse in one smooth, graceful motion.

"I wish you'd let me help you, stubborn woman." Mel dropped a kiss on his wife's nose.

Lacie clung to his side. "I'm not made of glass."

Had Lacie worked through her fears?

Could Rayna?

"Congratulations." Clay slapped Mel on the back.

"How far along?" Rayna asked.

"Two months." Lacie rubbed her flat stomach.

That meant when Rayna had first met her, Lacie was already pregnant. And fear still ruled.

Clay pointed an accusing finger. "Been keeping secrets."

"We had some things"—Mel rubbed the back of his neck—"to work through."

Clay nodded. "Did you see anyone on the way out? Her brother and her friend are somewhere around here."

"I didn't see anyone." Lacie grinned. "You had a shoot today, didn't you? How's the ad campaign coming?"

"At full tilt," Clay drawled.

"Girls all over the country will be heading for the rodeo once they get a load of Clay." Lacie patted his cheek.

He actually blushed. "It's not that kind of campaign."

"Maybe not, but the results will be the same. When you got it, you got it, hon. And you've definitely got it."

Rayna tried to contain her laughter as Clay squirmed.

More approaching hoofbeats announced Gabby and Adam's arrival.

"Hey, we were wondering 'bout y'all." Clay dragged a dry limb into the center of the clearing. "Since y'all enjoyed the rodeo the other night, I got tickets for Friday night."

"Sounds great." Adam helped stack brush in a pile. "Could we bring the camera crew?"

Clay's jaw clenched. "Sure."

As the sun's descent painted the sky in pinks and oranges, the men added to the woodpile. Soon the fire blazed, while the women emptied the saddlebag and set up the food. Adam added another log and sparks flew then disintegrated into nothing.

The flickering glow lit the circle of friends. Probably a good thing, the way things had headed earlier. Watching a spectacular sunset alone with Clay? Not a good idea.

She glanced his way only to find him staring. Her gaze darted away. Could she trust herself with this guy? Even though he represented a lifestyle she wanted nothing to do with, a glance from those gorgeous green eyes threatened to melt her into a puddle. And he brought out the kid in her. The kid whose joy for life had been snuffed out after her mother left.

"Browned or blackened?"

Rayna jumped.

Clay stood beside her. "Sorry, didn't mean to startle you. How do you like your hot dog roasted?"

"Browned."

He fixed her a plate, and she headed over by Gabby, away from Clay.

"How many acres do you have, Clay?" Gabby asked.

"Two hundred, at the moment."

At the moment. Was he thinking of selling the ranch? Why? Why did she care?

The men moved on to dessert. Marshmallows sizzled and with a whoosh burst into flame. Kind of like her heart did when Clay got too close.

⁂

Midweek and entirely too early in the morning, she neared Lake Ray Hubbard with Adam, Gabby, and Kendra in pursuit of the photographer's brainstorm. The crew followed in a company van.

After a week of photo sessions in the studio, graphic design, and copy approval, finally an outdoor shoot. If only it weren't so early.

"So what does the lake have to do with cowboys?" Rayna covered her mouth to yawn.

"Just wait." Kendra smirked. "You'll see my vision when we get there. I just hope our model will comply."

"Nothing gratuitous. He's the CBR World Champ now."

"Whatever." Kendra waved an unconcerned hand.

Clay waited on the beach. His shiny mocha-colored horse with a black mane and tail stood beside his horse trailer. A large section of Windsurf Bay Park was deserted, closed to the public for the shoot. Early November was probably too chilly for beachgoers anyway.

Clay joked with the crew, just as down-to-earth as ever. Was he really that humble? She wanted to congratulate him on his title but didn't want to encourage him to continue in the reckless profession.

The crew got to work. Per instructions, Clay mounted the horse and guided it near the water. With sun-kissed waves in the background, Rayna caught Kendra's vision. The pictures were great. Especially with Clay the focus.

"Okay, now get off the horse and walk beside it."

"Her. This here's Mandy, and do you have any idea what sand and water do to a pair of CWW snakeskins?"

"Take them off then." Kendra rolled her eyes. "Can you please work with me here? Rayna, get his boots."

Rayna's smart low-heeled pumps already had sand crusted along the sides. She slipped off her shoes and trouser socks, rolled up her pant legs, and sank her bare toes into the cold, damp sand.

"Socks, too."

Clay stuffed his socks in his boots, handed them to her, and rewarded her with a smile. A wave rolled in around their bare feet, stealing Rayna's breath.

The chilly water soaked the legs of his CWW jeans up to his knees. "Whew. Kind of nippy."

They'd probably end up with pneumonia, but the pictures would be as gorgeous as the cowboy.

"Now walk along with the horse," Kendra called. "Perfect. You were born for this. Now lose the shirt."

"No," Clay snapped. "I told you, no beefcake."

"What if I told you your contract requires it?"

He threw his head back and laughed. "Lady, I'm not stupid. I read the contract. If it had mentioned anything about losing my shirt, I wouldn't have signed. Now, I'll work with you fine, but with my Cowboy Western Wear shirt on— the way my sponsor intended."

Silence ruled the battle of wills. Finally, Kendra sighed.

Clay grinned.

The rest of the shoot went off without a hitch, except for the hitch he put in Rayna's heart.

Why did he have to be so perfect? Committed to Christ, honorable, loyal, moral—all the things she'd want in a man— if she were looking. Clay would fully commit and never leave his wife for another woman. The perfect man—except he rode bulls for a living.

❧

Friday night, rodeo night at the Stockyards. What was she doing looking forward to a rodeo? A horn honked. Rayna rushed to the window of her condo to see Clay get out of the truck. She ran to the door, flung it open, and willed herself not to leap into his arms. He'd traveled a lot lately and she'd barely seen him, but she shouldn't be missing him.

"Hey, little filly, you sure are pretty in pink."

She frowned. Was he color blind? Her blouse was decidedly emerald.

"Your cheeks."

Her face warmed more, and he gently chucked her nose.

"Shouldn't we have left earlier?"

"I signed up already. I'm in the second bull round, so I don't have to be there until steer roping."

"Why are you still competing when you're already the CBR World Champion?"

"I'm still in the running for the Stockyards Finals."

"But why bother?"

"I started at the Stockyards. It's where I rose through the ranks. It's kind of like home, keeps me in bull-riding shape, and I hope to inspire some kid just starting out."

Yeah, he was too perfect.

Thankfully, Clay kept the small talk impersonal during the hour drive.

As they entered the coliseum, the rodeo queen rode around the arena with a sponsor flag. Barely any dust stirred.

"Why is it dustier at your outside arena than inside? It seems it would be the opposite."

"It's a special mixture for indoor sites since the dust's got nowhere to go. The elements have 'bout worn mine down to plain ol' dirt, but I'm working on it." Clay pointed toward the entrance. "There's Adam and Gabby."

Rayna shook her head. "Uh-uh, I don't want to intrude on their date. I think I'll find Lacie."

"Shouldn't you hang with the camera crew?" His jaw clenched.

"They know what they're doing. I'll just give final approval for what we present to you."

She nibbled on the inside of her lip. "Why aren't you

comfortable with them being here?"

"Most of these guys aren't pros. Cameras might make some of them nervous, or try to show off. I don't like mixing business with work. And I don't wanna be some hunk of the month either." He took off his hat and ran his fingers through his hair with a groan. "I hate this whole thing."

"Why?"

"I don't want to be a household name." He shrugged. "I'm just a cowboy, a businessman, the guy next door."

If you say so. She'd never met a swoon-worthy guy next door before. "Then why did you agree to be the spokesman for CWW and have them hire my firm?"

"My ranch hit a slump and my injury last year cut into my finances. I couldn't afford to lose my sponsor."

"You won't lose the ranch, will you?" She touched his arm.

"No, but I was on the verge of laying some people off. And I didn't wanna do that. Most of my employees have families. They depend on the ranch for income. I needed CWW to keep backing me so I could get to Colorado and win, so I could keep my ranch hands. Now I'm stuck keeping my end of the bargain. Just be sure none of this comes out with a beefcake slant, will you?" He blushed.

"I'll try." But it wouldn't be easy. He was beefcake without even trying.

"Do better than try."

As time for the second round of bulls neared, the stands filled with spectators. Why would this many people show up? Willingly?

"Clay, thanks for inviting me." Kendra launched herself in his path. "I'm so excited. My first Clay Warren rodeo."

Rayna frowned. Apparently the photographer had gotten over her battle of wills with the handsome cowboy.

"Can I get a picture before you get all dirty?" Kendra tucked her hair behind her ear.

Rayna's jaw dropped.

"Sure, if you must."

"Don't just stand there. Work it. Lean on the fence."

Clay rolled his eyes but dutifully propped one arm on the fence for a heart-stopping shot.

As the camera flashed, Natalie joined them.

"Clay, darling. There you are." She moved in for a hug, but he stepped aside.

"Good seeing you, but I gotta git." He turned to Rayna. "There's Lacie. See you later."

Lacie waved, and Rayna left the women alone.

"What's going on over there?" Lacie greeted her with a fond embrace. "Who's that woman?"

"Part of my camera crew. I think she'd like to give Natalie a run for her money."

"Don't let her move in on your territory, hon."

Rayna gasped. "Clay is not my territory."

"Maybe not, but he'd like to be. Why don't you take him up on it? Y'all would be perfect. That other one"—she waved her hand toward Kendra—"seems too forward for him."

"Now, that's one of the biggest understatements I've ever heard. How are you feeling?"

"Fine." Lacie pressed a hand to her stomach. "Except this poor baby is destined to be nervous every Friday and Saturday night. Want to get something to drink and hide out in the lobby until the roping's over?"

"Good idea. Can we hide there all night, except for the barrel racing?"

"I wouldn't mind at all. But I gotta support my man. It might be a good idea for you to stay back there during the bull riding though."

They rounded the coliseum toward the concession stands.

"No. I'll be fine. I've spent a lot of time around bulls lately. I'm getting used to it." She hadn't even used her inhaler before coming. She'd face life head-on, one bull at a time.

"Do you have to take pictures tonight?"

"No. I'm here for the show, I guess."

A group of women stood in a circle, but no Natalie. Rayna's tensed muscles relaxed. She wouldn't have to deal with the other woman's venom. Maybe Natalie would focus on Kendra as her true adversary. If the rivals knew Clay at all, they'd realize neither one of them had a chance.

This time, she got their drinks while Lacie visited with the other wives and girlfriends. Rayna joined the circle as they swapped pregnancy, kid, and husband stories. Though she laughed in all the right places, she was out of place as usual in Clay's world. She sipped her bottled water while everyone else drank sweet tea. As the evening progressed, a few of the women left to prepare for upcoming events.

"We'd better get back." Lacie tossed her empty cup in the trash. "Roping's over."

As they made their way to the arena, they stepped around a man in a wheelchair.

"Why Dusty, you're a sight for sore eyes. We've missed you." Lacie hugged the man then the stocky woman with him.

"Thanks for all the cards, Lacie." The woman squeezed her hand. "It meant a lot, especially the ones from the church. We might just come visit sometime."

"Oh, please do. You could even ride with Mel and me."

"Y'all's truck wouldn't accommodate Dusty's chair."

"Then maybe we could come ride with y'all. Let's do that. I'll call you to make plans."

The woman looked uncertain. "Okay."

"Good seeing you."

Lacie turned back to Rayna and whispered as they continued on their way. "Sorry I didn't introduce you, but I can't for the life of me remember her name."

"What happened to him?"

"Bull riding. Last year."

Oh, for a tranquilizer. Maybe she should have used her inhaler, but she felt like such a wimp. Rayna shuddered. "Will he walk again?"

"Oh yeah. He had a head injury, so lots of therapy. But he's doing real good. If I know Dusty, he'll be riding again by next season. Mel and Clay have witnessed to him for years, and I finally roped them right into church. Did you see her face? Well, she's not getting out of it now. Nope. No way."

They hurried back to their seats.

"Ladies and Gentlemen," the announcer's voice boomed over the speaker. "And now for one of the buckingest events of the evening. They're rough, they're ready, and they're willing. It's time for our second round of bull riding."

Six cowboys fell before the buzzer, but the bullfighters did their jobs well, and no one was hurt. One man got his hand caught in the rope. Dangling from the mammoth bull's side, he bounced and spiraled until finally the pick-up man managed to get him loose.

By the time the gate burst open, with Clay straddling a colossal black monster, she'd worked herself into a frenzy of dread. Her stomach knotted.

The bull twisted, spun, and jerked. Though Clay took each jolt in stride, something large and heavy settled on Rayna's chest. Her breath wouldn't come.

"Rayna?" Lacie called.

From far away.

Rayna's three-year-old feet dangled as she sat in her mother's lap. Mom's muscles went taut, her gaze glued to the cowboy. He fell and the bull went after him. Mom screamed. Rayna did, too.

The clown distracted the black bull. For a moment. Mom's fear choked Rayna's breath. The bull turned back toward the cowboy, methodically pawing the ground before it charged. Someone screamed, bloodcurdling and desperate.

seven

Back in the stands, Rayna realized the sound came from her constricted throat. Clay leaped from the bull, somehow remained upright, and ran with the creature in pursuit. As two thousand pounds of fury reached him, Clay climbed the fence and jumped over to safety. Tears blurred her vision.

"Sorry for digging in your purse, but here." Lacie jabbed Rayna's inhaler in her face.

Rayna coughed and sucked in two puffs, but she still couldn't get air.

"I'm calling Clay." Lacie's voice sounded nearer. "You hang in there, hon."

But she still couldn't breathe. The driving beat of a rock song ended, and for a moment, she could hear her own raspy, hacking struggle.

After a few minutes, her coughing let up, the pressure lessened, and air filled her lungs.

"You're gettin' better." Lacie patted her shoulder.

Clay ran into the stands, and nearing her seat, he knelt beside her, his eyes filled with worry. "Did you call an ambulance?" He tenderly stroked her cheek.

"No. She's better. It's an asthma attack, and she took her medicine." Lacie blew out a breath as if she'd been holding it. "A lot better. You should have seen her a few minutes ago."

"Should we call an ambulance, darlin'?"

The weight on her chest had eased, and Rayna shook her head. "Better," she gasped.

"I'll take her." Clay tried to pick her up.

"No." Her hands clamped onto the edge of her seat. "Please, I don't want to make any more of a scene than I already have. Just help me walk."

He nodded and helped her stand. "Steady. Keep breathing,

darlin'. You'll be fine. Thanks, Lacie."

She clung to him as they descended the stands. His mere presence provided comfort, and her breath came easier.

As they took the back exit, Clay gently lifted her into his arms and effortlessly carried her to his truck.

Her airflow was almost normal.

He set her inside. "I'll lay the seat back."

"No, I'm okay." An odd wheezing gasp escaped, and her face warmed. He'd never want to take her anywhere again.

"We'll sit here awhile. Just relax. Lean on me." He got in the driver's side and pulled her against his shoulder.

"Could we get away from here?"

"Sure." He started the engine and backed the truck out.

Silence invaded the cab, and she didn't pay any attention to where he headed. Sightlessly, she stared out the window. *Breathing normal. Everything's okay.*

"Want to talk about what happened back there?"

What had she remembered? Who was the cowboy? Did he die? She gasped, and her heart sped up.

"Never mind. Just breathe."

The only sound was her steady inhale and exhale.

"Want me to stop and get you anything?"

Feeling stronger, she replied, "No. This is so embarrassing. Just take me home."

"Asthma isn't anything to be embarrassed about, and you're in no shape to be alone."

"My dad's then. Take me to my dad's house."

"It's late. Almost eleven."

"I have a key, and besides, Daddy's a night owl." And surely his woman friend would be gone by now.

"Okay. Lay your seat back and tell me where."

❧

Her breathing eased even more. Clay glanced over to make sure she hadn't passed out. Fast asleep. Poor gal was exhausted.

What on earth had triggered the attack? Allergy to dust, bulls, horses? Lacie said it started during his bull ride. Surely she hadn't panicked over that. Though he was falling for her, could she feel so strongly about him that a bull ride could take her breath away? A nice thought, but no, it went deeper than that. He'd seen complete, utter terror in her eyes.

He pulled into the drive of a neat, contemporary house with a large front porch.

Wake her up? After the evening she'd had? But he didn't want to deliver her to the door of the wrong house. The mailbox read DR. NICK LANDERS. Right last name, but she'd never mentioned anything about her dad being a doctor. Gently, he shook her.

"Rayna."

Her eyelids flew open.

"It's me. Everything's okay. We're at your dad's. I think. Just wanted to make sure this is the right place."

"This is it. Thanks for bringing me." She fumbled for the door latch.

"Hey, wait up. Let me get that for you." He hurried out the driver's side and around to her.

Wobbly. He steadied her.

"Let me carry you."

"No, I'm okay. Just exhausted."

"I'll carry you."

"No. What will my father think if some guy he's never met carries me in?"

"Point taken. Where does he hang out this time of night?"

"His study in the back of the house."

"Okay, how about I carry you inside, then I'll prop you up somewhere before you call your dad?"

Weak as a newborn foal, she handed him the key.

He scooped her up and headed to the porch.

Inside the door, a man stood waiting, his face as red as his daughter's hair.

"Rayna, I thought I heard something. Are you all right?"

Shaking her head, she started to cry.

"Young man, what have you done to my daughter?"

"Nothing, Daddy. Clay brought me home."

"If you'll tell me where to put her, I'll explain, sir."

"I'll take her."

"Oh, for goodness' sake, I can walk. Put me down, Clay."

Unwilling to upset her again, he set her down. As she staggered toward the pale green couch, her father steadied her despite her protests. After pulling a throw over her, he turned back toward Clay.

"Young man, you've got some explaining to do."

Clay swallowed hard. "My name's Clay Warren. Your daughter's been working on an ad campaign for me. I'm a bull rider, and she had an asthma attack at the rodeo."

With a worried frown, her father turned to Rayna.

Tears coursed down her cheeks.

"Oh Daddy," she sobbed.

Anger evaporated, the worried father sat beside his daughter and gathered her in his arms. "Did you take her to the emergency room?"

"No, sir." Clay tried to stay still, afraid his boots might scuff the hardwood floors. "By the time I got there, she'd taken her medicine and just wanted to go home. I didn't want to leave her alone at her place, so we came here instead."

"Thank you for bringing her home. I can handle things here."

"Yes, sir." Clay turned away.

"Thanks for taking care of me," Rayna managed through her tears.

"I'll check on you tomorrow. Get some rest."

❧

The door shut behind Clay.

Rayna sucked in a deep breath. "I remember being at the rodeo, Daddy. A long time ago."

"Shh. I was afraid of that. Let's get you to bed."

"No. I can't. Every time I close my eyes, I see—" she squeaked.

"Oh sweetheart. I'm so sorry." Daddy's shoulders slumped. "It seemed better if we didn't talk about it."

"Did he die?"

Daddy winced. "No, but I saw Dayle's reaction. She told me everything."

Rayna's insides twisted in a tight knot. "Told you what?"

He closed his eyes.

A sigh escaped him as he massaged the back of his neck. "I should have told you years ago."

૨&

Rayna blinked bleary eyes and stretched. A night-light lit her old bedroom. What was she doing here?

It all came back. Daddy had insisted she stay the night. So she could come to terms with stumbling upon the skeleton in her family closet. And in knowing what haunted her, everything made sense.

The digital clock cast a green glow: 3:11 a.m.

She sensed a presence in the room and squinted toward the rocking chair in the corner. A figure sat there, still, silent. She reached for the lamp. "Daddy?"

Light chased darkness from the room. A wide-eyed woman sat in the chair.

Rayna gasped.

A woman she'd dreamed of, a woman she'd remembered vividly at the rodeo.

"You?"

"I—I thought you'd sleep through the night."

"What are you doing here?"

"I wanted to make sure you were okay."

"Rayna?" Daddy stepped in the doorway.

Rayna pointed an accusing finger at her mother. "Why is she here?"

Daddy's eyes widened. "Dayle, I thought you left."

"I just wanted to—"

"She's much too upset. Dayle, please go home."

Rayna flung the covers back, glad she'd gone to bed fully clothed. "She can stay. I'm leaving."

"Rayna, please." Daddy blocked her exit.

"Why didn't you tell me?"

"I wasn't sure how."

"Telling me would have been better than me waking up to her lurking in the corner." She tried to get past him.

"I don't think you're in any shape to drive, and you don't have your car."

Rayna hissed out a sigh. "Then I'll walk."

"No." He gently gripped her shoulders. "We'll get out of your hair and I'll call Adam to drive you home."

Daddy ushered her mother out the door.

Her mother who'd abandoned her at three.

Rayna sank onto the bed and covered her face with her hands.

๛

Rayna plodded to the kitchen. Maybe caffeine would help settle her fidgets. Thank goodness it was Saturday. At least, after a sleepless night, she didn't have to worry about work.

A man stood at her sink.

Stumbling back, she screamed.

Adam whirled around. "It's me."

Clutching a hand to her heart, she squeaked, "What are you doing here?"

"I slept on the couch. Didn't think you should be alone. Want to talk?"

Rayna pressed her fingers to trembling lips.

Adam's arms came around her. "It's okay. Maybe later."

"I guess I know why you didn't like Clay at first."

"I was wrong about him. He's nothing like Lefty Shelton." Adam spat the name as if it left a bitter aftertaste.

Shock waves coursed through her. "Did you know—did you know she was in town?"

"No. Not until Dad called me to come get you."

"Why is she back? Why now?"

"I don't know." Adam shook his head. "But it doesn't matter. We don't need her. We never have."

๛

Clay shifted his weight from one foot to the other then rang the bell. Minutes passed, floorboards creaked, and her father opened the door. He looked tired. More lines in his face than the night before. He frowned then stepped outside. "Yes?"

"I'd like to see Rayna."

"Adam drove her home last night."

"Is she okay?"

"For the most part."

"Sir, I know you probably think it's none of my business, but I care very deeply 'bout your daughter. I'd like to know what happened last night. Maybe I can help."

Dr. Landers closed his eyes, rubbing the back of his neck with one hand. "A long-ago accident blew this family apart. Rayna was a small child and suppressed the memories. They surfaced last night."

"Does she need help? I mean, professional help."

"I'm a psychologist."

"That's good to know." Clay cleared his throat. "I'm just a cowboy, but I care. Maybe I can help Rayna, by being there for her, if nothing else."

"She told me you're a strong Christian."

"Yes, sir."

"I knew of a bull rider once through a mutual acquaintance, fellow by the name of Ty Warren."

"My daddy."

"You look like him. A fine man. I wouldn't trust just any young man with my daughter."

"You can count on me, sir."

Dr. Landers squeezed his shoulder. "Don't push her. She may not be ready to talk yet. Give her time."

"Is it Rayna?" A woman stepped into view. An older version of Rayna. Her faded auburn, chin-length hair framed the same amber eyes, red-rimmed and puffy. No freckles.

"I'm sorry, I should have called. Here's my card." Clay handed it to him and tipped his hat.

"I'll give you a call." Dr. Landers shut the door in his face.

❧

The doorbell rang. Rayna rolled her eyes. Not in the mood for company. Probably Daddy.

She adjusted the plush teal robe, tied the belt, and hurried to the door to peer through the peephole. *Clay.* She gasped.

"Rayna, I know you're here. Just wanted to check on you."

"You were supposed to call."

"Can I come in?"

"I'm not dressed." No makeup, with red, puffy eyes, and hair decidedly undone.

"Just get decent, and let me in."

"Why don't you come back later? I'm not. . .presentable."

"I don't care what you look like. I'm not leaving till I make sure you're okay. Your neighbors are getting curious."

With a sigh, she opened the door, but he wasn't there. She stuck her head out to find him leaning against the siding. No nosy neighbors.

"I don't see anyone."

"I didn't say they were checking yet, but they will be if we keep hollering back and forth."

"Are you coming in?"

"You're beautiful." He followed her inside.

"And you're crazy."

"I'm worried about you."

Me too.

He pulled her into his arms. "You okay?"

"Sort of."

"I stopped by your dad's first."

"You did?" She stiffened.

"He said you're dealing with major stuff. Whatever it is, I thought it might help if I was here for you."

Tears burned her eyes, and she relaxed against him. "That's very sweet, but—"

"How about breakfast?"

"I'm not in the mood to cook, and I'm not presentable enough to go out."

"Not you, silly gal. I'll cook."

"Oh. I'm not even sure what I have."

He pulled away. Despite her well-laid plans of not falling for him, she would've rather stayed in his arms than eat.

"I brought my own. Be right back." He hurried out.

Could she run to the bathroom and put herself together quickly? No amount of cosmetics would help this morning.

A soft tap on the door and Clay came in with a grocery sack. "You sit a spell. Relax and I'll see what I can rustle up. Kitchen through here?"

She nodded and watched him disappear then curled into a ball on the couch, knees pulled to her chest. Soon the smell of bacon wafted through the air. Her stomach growled.

Fifteen minutes later, Clay came back carrying a tray she'd forgotten she had. He set it in her lap. Not only bacon but scrambled eggs and biscuits, too. From the adjoining dining room, he grabbed a chair, brought it over beside her, turned it around backward, and straddled it.

She sipped the grape juice. "How did you know I love grape juice, and this is the only way I eat eggs?"

"I didn't, but I hate orange juice. It's—"

"Bitter." They echoed each other.

"And it oughta be a crime to do anything to an egg other than scramble it."

More common ground. "I never eat like this. I usually have coffee and a bran muffin."

"You don't have anything to worry about. You're. . .perfect."

"I wouldn't put it that way exactly, but I like to be healthy, watch what I eat, and exercise."

"You look great."

Her skin heated until she was certain even her hair blushed. She must look a sight. But it didn't matter. This would be the last time she saw him. *Just enjoy being with him.*

"Let's pray, and then you can dig in." He took off his hat and claimed her hand. "Heavenly Father, we ask that You be with Rayna and her family. Comfort them. Provide guidance and peace. We thank You for this food and for bringing us into each other's lives. Amen."

The bacon was just right, not too crispy, but nice and done. She savored each bite.

"What are your plans for the day?"

"Pull myself together and have dinner with my brother tonight. Convince him I'm fine and pretend everything's okay." Her voice cracked.

"What if I go with you? You know, moral support. I'm an expert at keeping things light."

She averted her gaze from the intensity of his green eyes. "It was really nice of you to come over. But I'm not sure. . ." *About you being anywhere in my life.* "Maybe we should just leave it at working together."

"But we're about to wrap up the campaign. When it's over, we could still see each other, couldn't we?"

Her heart skipped a beat. "I'm in such turmoil right now. I don't want to drag you into that."

"You don't have to drag me. I believe I'm already here. By choice." He touched her hand.

She pulled away. "Most guys would run the other way, and right now, I think that's what you should do. My whole life changed last night. I found out things I'd tried hard not to know." She shook her head with a quivery sigh.

Clay ran his fingers through his tousled curls. "I'm sure whatever this is about, your folks love you."

"My mother left years ago." She pressed her fist to her lips.

He moved the tray, sat beside her, and pulled her into his arms.

eight

Minutes passed before Rayna could speak again. "You've been great, but you should go." She pushed away from him.

Clay traced her cheek with gentle fingertips. "I don't want to leave you. I'd like to help you through this. I promise not to ask any questions. You can fill me in if and when you want to."

She shook her head. "I'm sorry, Clay, but I can't deal with you right now. There's too much else going on."

Hurt clouded his eyes, and he stood. "I didn't realize I was so difficult to deal with. I'm trying to help."

"I know and I really appreciate it, but right now I have to sort some things out."

He knelt in front of her and took both of her hands in his. "I don't understand your take on this. Seems we got a good thing going here, and you need someone to lean on. But if this is what you want, I'll go."

"It is." She managed to control her voice. No quiver, though she couldn't look at him.

"I'll be around, Rayna. If you need me, you know where to find me." He stood and turned to leave. "I don't give up easily."

Her gaze dropped to the floor and she closed her eyes. Couldn't bear to watch him go. The door closed and she pressed a hand to quivery lips. With certainty, she knew the best thing that had ever happened to her had walked away. Because she told him to.

છે

When had Rayna's mom reentered the premises? Had she come back because Rayna learned the truth? Whatever that truth was.

No wonder Rayna had sent him away. She was dealing not only with suppressed memories but with her mother's return.

Clay stepped inside the ranch house and hung his hat on the peg behind the door. Stretching from side to side, he tried to work out the knots and kinks the bull had inflicted on him last night.

The private dining room door burst open to reveal his beaming parents.

His chest swelled at the sparkle in Dad's eyes. He'd lived up to the legend that was his father. For this year anyway.

Mom pounced on him. "There's my three-time CBR World Champ. I'm still getting used to the sound of it. Oh, doll baby, you're rhythm in motion with the bull every time you ride."

"Takes after his pappy." His dad clapped him on the shoulder.

Mom closed her eyes. "Lots of praying every time you ride."

"Couldn't help but notice a certain extra redhead at the Stockyards last night." Dad chuckled. "You sure made a beeline to her after your ride."

"She's my creative director for the ad campaign."

"I think there's a bit more to it." Mom elbowed him and turned toward the kitchen. "Lunch is almost on."

"What's wrong, son?" Dad sank into the couch and propped his feet on the raw-pine coffee table. "You look like you lost your best horse."

"Nothing. Rough night."

"You were gone before me and your mama got here this morning. What was your all-fired hurry? Is it that girl?"

"Sort of." Clay shrugged. "Hey, did you ever know a guy by the name of Nick Landers?"

Dad scratched his head. "Nick Landers. Hmm, Nick Landers. Sounds familiar."

"He said you met through a mutual acquaintance. Seems to think highly of you."

Pain threaded its way through Dad's features. "I remember." He cleared his throat and got a handle on his emotions. "Where'd you run into Nick?"

"He's Rayna's father."

"You don't say. Small world, huh? Your mama's probably got lunch ready. Best head to the trough."

ð

Monday morning. More than anything, Rayna wanted to claim she was ill, go home, and stay in bed. For the rest of the day, the week, her life. Instead, she sat at her desk, staring at the lit screen, trying to concentrate on the graphics.

Gabby patiently waited for approval.

"I'll get back with you on this."

"Sure." Gabby stood. "Is anything wrong with the layout?"

"I'm sure it's fine. I'm just distracted this morning."

"Take your time. I'll come back later."

"Thanks." Rayna's fingers hovered over the keyboard for a moment. She typed in "Lefty Shelton," clicked on the first site that popped up, then clicked PRINT. Scanning over the pages, Rayna stiffened. That's why her mom came crawling back. The cowboy died.

Someone stopped in her open doorway.

Clay.

Her heart did a flip-flop, and she closed her browser.

"Can we talk in private?"

"This really isn't necessary." Rayna stuffed the papers in the bottom of her briefcase.

"Yes, it is."

He didn't give up easily. Instead, he shut the door. "Listen, why don't you tell them to get a new art director?"

"I can't do that."

"Why not? You'd be off the hook."

"I've never failed to finish a project, and I'm not going to start now."

"I'm worried about you." He touched her cheek.

She jerked away as if burned by fire. She didn't need any added complications, and he definitely was one. "Don't be. I'm fine."

Gently, he raised her chin until she had no choice but to look at him.

"There's something haunting in your eyes. It wasn't there

when we first met, and I put it there. I wish I'd never taken you to the rodeo, and I don't want to torment you with this campaign."

A steely resolve moved up her spine. She wasn't some crybaby who couldn't face life's hurdles.

She looked into his eyes with all the intensity she could muster. "It's very sweet of you to be concerned, but I'm fine. Now, if you'll excuse me, I have work to do." She turned her back on him.

Thankfully, he took the hint. The door opened and his footsteps faded away.

❧

Clay watched Lacie finishing up a riding lesson with a seven-year-old boy. She had a way with horses and kids. In the beginning, the boy had barely been able to sit astride the pinto pony. Now he rode like a natural. Lacie hugged the child and turned him over to his parents.

"You know if you ever need a break, you're tired, or your back hurts, you can take a day off."

"I'm fine. How's Rayna?"

"A mess."

"What on earth happened the other night? It sure seemed like more than asthma."

"Her dad said she remembered something awful that happened a long time ago. I think it's something to do with her mom. She left when Rayna was a kid."

"Oh, that poor girl."

"I went to talk to her dad to see if he thinks she can handle finishing up the details on the ad campaign. I mean, mentally. Turns out he's a psychologist."

"And he said?" Lacie climbed the fence to perch on the top rail.

"Nothing. Her mom was there. I don't know when she came back, but I don't think Rayna's handling her return well." His cell vibrated and he dug it from his pocket. "Clay Warren here."

"It's Nick Landers, Rayna's father."

Clay waved at Lacie and turned toward the ranch.

"Yes, thanks for getting back with me, sir. I'm sorry about the other day. Shoulda called first."

"It's okay. What did you need to speak to me about?"

"I've got a dilemma."

"Concerning Rayna?"

"Yes, sir. She won't let me help her. Basically told me to get lost. In the meantime, I've got her in a pickle."

"How's that?"

"We still have to finish up the ad campaign. As art director, she'll have to be present at the photo shoots. Bull-riding photo shoots." Clay heard a sigh. "I tried to get her to let them assign a different art director, but she refused. Says she can handle it."

"Sounds like my stubborn, redheaded daughter."

"What I want to know, sir, is can she handle it?"

"I'm not sure. I'll talk to her about it and get back with you."

"I'm willing to break the contract if needed, sir." He turned his chair toward the window where he could barely see the clearing. The future site of his dream cabin. With the woman he loved. Rayna.

"I appreciate that. One thing I do know, Rayna is strong. She'll be fine."

"That's good to know, sir. Good to know."

❧

The phone on Rayna's desk rang. An outside call. *Clay?*

"Bradley & Associates. Rayna Landers speaking. How may I help you?"

"Rayna, please don't hang up," Daddy's voice pleaded.

"I'd never hang up on you." Okay, so maybe he'd held out on the truth, but he was her only constant. Him and Adam.

"I wanted to call sooner."

"I'm sorry I got so angry the other night." She stood at her office window. The city below crawled with tiny cars and people while the Dallas horizon reflected the sun's rays in endless skyscraper windows. "You should have told me."

"I know."

"Is she still in town?"

"Yes." A slight pause. "Clay stopped by the other day. He's worried about this project being too hard on you. That boy really cares about you, sweetie."

The lump in her throat prevented any response.

"He's willing to cancel the contract if you need him to."

Movement in the hall. Gabby hesitated a moment then moved on.

"That won't be necessary. I'm fine."

"I'd like you to come to the house."

Rayna closed her eyes. "Will she be there?"

"I was hoping we could all have a nice Thanksgiving meal together next week."

"I need to go." She hung up, closed her eyes, and took several deep breaths, then went looking for Gabby.

☙

After the long Thanksgiving weekend, Rayna stood at the fence of Clay's arena again. Calm, cool, and collected. She didn't even hide behind the stands but faced the challenge head-on. As the sun began its slow descent, the floodlights hummed to life with a steady buzz, growing brighter as they gained strength.

Grit coated her skin, hair, and clothing as a chilly wind swirled dust tornadoes up into the darkening sky and hovered around the lights like a foreboding cloud. *Please let the still shots and footage be enough to finish the project.*

"Thanks, everybody. Good work." She sat on the bottom bleacher. It was over.

"The photo crew is going back to the office, but they don't have room for you," Gabby called. "Adam and I will take you back before we go to dinner."

"I'll give Rayna a ride," Clay called.

"Thanks." Adam shook Clay's hand.

Traitor.

Vehicles cleared out and minutes later they were alone. Mental note: *If there's a next time, bring my car.*

"You were a real trooper today." Clay dusted himself off. "Today didn't seem to faze you."

"Daddy had my doctor up my dosage."

He grabbed her arm. "You had to get drugged up to handle this shoot? Okay, that's it. I'm getting a different art director."

"I'm not drugged up!" She jerked away.

"Typical doctor. They think drugs fix everything."

She jabbed a finger at him. "Leave Daddy out of this."

"I'm sorry. I don't like drugs. Got a lot of good friends who ended up hooked on tranquilizers."

"It's asthma medication. FYI, asthmatics can't take tranquilizers." She stalked toward his truck. "Just take me to the office."

Without protest, he hurried toward the passenger's side.

"And I can get my own door." She yanked it open and climbed inside, as far away from him as she could get.

"You know, I'm a good listener. And I certainly didn't mean to disrespect your father. I honestly want to help you handle whatever the problem is. I care enough about you to want you to be happy, whether I'm included in the equation or not."

She swallowed hard.

"Can I just hold you? Comfort. That's all I'm offering."

She laid her head on his much-needed shoulder. "I'm sorry I overreacted." *It's just that I'm half mad at Daddy right now.*

"It's okay. One of these days, I'll learn to pick my words better." He wrapped his arms around her. "Ah, now this is nice."

"I didn't go to my father's house for Thanksgiving, and when he called, I didn't answer."

"I wish I'd have known—you could've come to my folks'."

"Adam didn't go either, so I cooked us a meal." Why was she telling him all this? "I shouldn't be here."

"I agree. We'll get a different art director."

"No, I mean, with you." She burrowed deeper into his shoulder. "I'm very sure I could fall head over heels for you."

"No pressure. We can take things slow. 'Cuz that 'head over heels' thing—right back at you, darlin'."

"But I can't do the rodeo thing."

"You don't have to go ever again."

"That wouldn't be right. It's part of you. You need to find someone who can support you in doing what you love."

"I'd rather have someone to love than someone to support me in the rodeo. And I'm definitely falling for you."

"I can't deal with worrying about something happening to you. I don't want to end up like Lacie—pregnant and terrified her husband will die."

"You don't want kids, so how could you end up like her?" He stroked her hair.

"I figured out why I've never wanted kids."

"Why?"

"I can't talk about it. Yet. But if I could get all of this worked out, it might change how I feel about children."

"Can you even have kids with your asthma?"

"Some women's symptoms improve during pregnancy. It's not considered high risk."

"Cast your cares upon Jesus."

His words sliced through her heart.

"Easier said than done." She pulled away from him. "I think we should go now."

"If that's what you want." He bit his lip. "Listen, I know it's bad timing, but CWW has set me up to do lots of promoting, and I've got commercials to film for them and for GAC. 'Fraid I'll be tied up for a couple of weeks."

I'll miss you.

"When things settle down, I want you to meet my pastor, Brother Timothy."

"I have my own pastor."

"Yes, but my pastor is a counselor. Maybe he could help."

She laughed. "My father is a psychologist."

"Look, don't take this the wrong way, but maybe your dad is too close to the situation." He held up his hand as if to ward off a blow.

She pushed his hand down. "What do you mean?"

"I don't mean anything against your dad. He's doing the best he can, but maybe he's too close to you to help. Maybe someone who's not emotionally invested could help you work through things."

"Someone detached."

"Think about it while I'm gone."

She nodded as a knot clogged her throat.

❧

The two weeks without Clay dragged by. And his absence made her heart grow fonder. On the Net, she followed his triumphs. He was still in the lead for the Stockyards Finals with Mel leading the bronc standings. She was even tempted to watch for his commercials and rodeos on GAC.

By the time he'd finally called to see if she planned to attend church with him, she couldn't agree fast enough.

Sunday morning, her doorbell rang. She ran to the door, flung it open, and hurled herself into Clay's arms.

"Wow, now that's some kind of welcome," he drawled.

No. That's some kind of I missed you.

Clay escorted her to the truck and carefully kept the small talk ranch-focused. Almost an hour later, he pulled in at an old-style church.

Though cozy and filled with friendly people, Rayna sat in the young adult class, trying to keep her mind on the Bible instead of the attractive teacher, Clay. A few of the other women seemed to have the same problem.

After class, he took her hand in his and steered her back toward the sanctuary.

Her pulse launched into overdrive. "Good lesson."

"Hope so. For some reason, I had a hard time concentrating this morning. This is where I always sit. I'm an usher, so I'll be busy for a while. Save me a seat." He hurried to the back of the church.

"Rayna, aren't you a sight for sore eyes." Ty gave her a quick hug followed by the same greeting from his wife.

"So you're the girl who's been keeping our boy so busy." Durlene grinned.

Rayna's face warmed. The pianist began playing a hymn. Everyone quieted and found seats. Obviously, Clay's boldness came from both sides. The song service began, and she didn't see him again until he helped take up the offering. Then, finally, he returned and claimed the seat between her and his mother.

The pastor delivered a fiery sermon promising insurance through the free gift of Jesus Christ. Several went to the altar afterward. More than Rayna had ever seen in her own church.

After the closing prayer, the crowd dispersed toward the exit, and Clay introduced her to several people.

"Are you two going to lunch with us?" Durlene linked arms with Rayna.

"Nonsense. We'd cramp their style." Ty winked and escorted his wife toward their car.

"They're rather overwhelming. I hope they didn't scare you off." Clay slipped her hand in the crook of his arm and headed to his truck.

"They're nice. A bit bold, but I'm getting used to that."

"Brother Timothy wants to meet you at six thirty tomorrow night."

"I didn't expect it to be so soon." Her stomach fluttered.

"He wants to help. Just think about it. In the meantime, how about lunch?"

"I promised to meet Adam."

"Still afraid of me?"

"He's worried about me, and I'm not sure about spending all this time together. I—"

He pressed his finger to her lips. "Lunch tomorrow? Two friends having lunch."

"That sounds nice."

"How about the Cheesecake Factory? What time should I pick you up from work?"

Kendra would have a field day since she didn't get anywhere with Clay. "That would be out of your way. Let me meet you."

"I thought you trusted me."

"I do. I'm trying to save you some time and trouble."

"I'd walk over fiery coals for you."

Her cheeks heated. "You don't *really* know me."

"I like what I do know. Okay, we'll meet for lunch. And I'll drive you to the church tomorrow night."

"That's not necessary. It could be awhile, and I don't want you having to wait for me."

"It was Brother Timothy's idea. He doesn't like anyone to drive home from a counseling session alone. What about Saturday night?"

"Pretty confident, are you? What if Monday's lunch doesn't go well?"

"I don't see that happening."

She smiled for the first time since the rodeo. "Okay. Oh. No, wait. Saturday night is my company Christmas party."

"It's only mid-December."

"They always have it early so it won't interfere with anyone's Christmas plans."

"Do you have a date?"

"Actually, no." Kendra, shmendra. "Would you like to come?"

"That's the best offer I've had in eons."

"Don't you have a rodeo?"

"I'm so far ahead in the Stockyards standing, I don't want to trounce the other guys, so I can afford a break."

❧

Somehow, Rayna and Clay had slipped out of the office underneath Kendra's radar. The waitress took their lunch orders and returned a few minutes later with their drinks. Soft music played in the background, and numerous diners surrounded them.

"Whew, there's nothing like a swig of sweet iced tea." Clay almost drained his glass and set it down. "Are you anxious about tonight?"

Rayna's stomach churned. "I shouldn't have ordered anything. I won't be able to eat it. I never can when I'm nervous."

He covered her hand with his. "Brother Timothy's really good."

"Have you ever had to see him?"

"No, but he helped my dad through a rough time. I was just a kid when one of my dad's friends from the rodeo died in a one-car accident. Fella by the name of Lefty Shelton."

Rayna gasped.

"Hey, you okay?"

"I remembered something I have to do at work."

"Surely it can wait till after lunch."

"It really can't. I'm sorry. I'll get a cab."

"I'll take you."

"That's not necessary. I don't want to ruin your lunch. Let me pay for mine."

"Ma'am." Clay stopped the waitress. "I need to pay now and come back for our food. Can you put our meals in to-go boxes?"

"Of course. I'll get your ticket." She scurried away.

"I'm sorry."

"Guess lunch didn't go well after all."

"It's not you."

He grinned. "Then we're still on for Saturday night?"

She tried to muster up a smile, but the muscles around her mouth wouldn't work. "Yes."

❧

Rayna stared at her reflection in the bathroom mirror. She'd had a hard time ditching Clay and had probably hurt his feelings. Chivalrous as usual, he'd insisted on escorting her to her office. She'd claimed a needed trip to the ladies' room to get rid of him.

She peeked out the door. With no sign of him, she hurried to her office.

"Marge, can you hold my calls, please?"

"Sure."

She dug in the bottom of her briefcase. THE ULTIMATE COWBOY: LEFTY SHELTON, the headline read above a picture of a man astride a massive bull. The next shot was a close-up. Dark brown hair, chocolate eyes that crinkled at the corners, a wide grin. Much like his cousin—her father whom he'd betrayed.

Rayna ran her fingers over the article and forced herself to read. He'd died over twenty years ago. Her phone rang.

She jumped. "Yes?"

"I'm sorry to bother you, Ms. Landers, but a familiar cowboy brought you lunch."

She closed her eyes. "Is he still here?"

"No, ma'am, he left."

❧

Clay slipped Rayna's fingers in his as they entered the church. A gust of mid-December wind followed them inside. Her haunted eyes tugged at his heart.

"Hey, you okay?"

She shrugged. "Thanks for bringing lunch."

"No problem. Did you eat?"

"Actually, I did."

"Good. Tough business demands a full stomach." He put his arm around her shoulders, nestling her against his side.

She didn't pull away.

"You'll like Brother Timothy. He's easy to talk to. When you get to where you wanna talk, that is."

"I've never needed a counselor in my entire life."

"Sometimes life has a way of throwing things at you. I'll wait for you here."

She flashed him a weak grin and walked into the office alone.

Joan, the pastor's wife, waved at him and shut the door. While Rayna worked out her demons, he paced. Outside lights filtered through the frosted windows, giving the sanctuary an ethereal glow. He knelt at the altar.

"Dear Lord," he prayed aloud, "help Rayna through the counseling session. Give her strength to face whatever it is she needs to face, and help me to be there for her. Say the right things, do the right things. Help me to keep my mind off those gorgeous eyes and on her emotional well-being. I don't want my falling in love with her to complicate things for her. Ease the gap between us, Lord. Smooth the differences. Work things out for us if we're meant to be."

Words escaped him and after a while, he found himself simply kneeling in God's presence, knowing that his Lord knew his heart, fondest desires, and longings.

He heard something, whispered a hasty amen, and stood.

Brother Timothy waited at the back of the sanctuary.

"Where is she?" Clay checked his watch. An hour and a half had passed.

"Still in my office with Joan. Go be with her. Stay as long as you like."

"Is she all right?"

"She's emotional, but she'll be fine." Brother Timothy patted his shoulder then continued to the altar.

Rayna sat on the couch with her knees drawn to her chest and arms tucked around her legs. Had he done the right thing in bringing her here?

The pastor's wife knelt, holding Rayna's hand. Eager to provide comfort, he felt his heart hammering in his chest.

Joan finished praying and left them alone.

He eased in beside Rayna, and she curled into his arms.

"I'm here, darlin'." He ran his fingers through silken hair. "Maybe this wasn't such a good idea."

"No, it was. I feel better. I may not look like it, but I do." She laughed. Actually laughed.

Clay's taut nerve endings unfrazzled. "Good. You don't know how good it is to hear you laugh."

"You were right, Brother Timothy is very easy to talk to."

"That's good."

Her eyes sparkled with life. Something he hadn't seen since the rodeo. The pinched, haunted look was still there, but it had eased.

"Thank You, Lord."

"For what?"

"While you were in with Brother Timothy, I was praying you'd be all right."

Her smile widened. "Thanks. I feel better than I have in a while. You've been great through this whole thing, and I haven't always appreciated you."

Clay's attention moved to her lips, so close to his own. Soft and tempting. Fragile and vulnerable.

He cleared his throat and looked away. "How 'bout supper?"

"I'm not hungry, but we can stop and get you something."

"Then I'll take you to your dad's tonight. I hate to leave you alone."

"No." Rayna's eyes squeezed shut. "Just take me home. I need to tell you what's going on."

"You don't have to."

"I know, but I want to."

If she didn't stop looking at him like that, his control would snap and he'd rain sweet kisses over her face.

•

nine

As they walked across her condo parking lot, Clay claimed Rayna's hand.

For a moment, Rayna had thought he would kiss her back at the church. And she'd wanted him to. Right there in the church office.

A weight had lifted from her world. How had Daddy borne the pressure of it all these years?

"Listen, you're tired. You need to go to bed."

"Exhausted and sleepy are two different things. I'm wide awake. Come inside?"

"I wish I could sleep on your couch, but that wouldn't do. Maybe I'll just stay till you fall asleep."

Once inside, she curled up on the couch. "Want something to drink?"

"I'm fine, but you could probably use a tall drink of water."

"I'm sure I look horrible."

"You could never look any way but beautiful."

Warmth spread over her. Maybe with her face all blotchy, he hadn't noticed the blush.

"Think I'll go freshen up."

The bathroom mirror told the tale. Splotchy, puffy, and red. It was a bad, bad thing for a redhead to cry. Rayna pressed a cold cloth to her face and wiped away what was left of her makeup. Repairs wouldn't work at this stage. Clay had already seen her at her worst. And he was still here. Could there be hope for their future?

As she entered the living room, he handed her the biggest tumbler she owned, filled with ice water.

"Thanks." Drier than she realized, she took a long drink then set the remains on a coaster.

"You have a right to know what's going on."

"You don't have to tell me anything. I only wanna help you."

"What if I need to talk?"

"Don't you think maybe you've done enough talking for one day?"

"Clay." She touched his cheek. "I'm okay. Sit down."

He sat in a sleek red chair, while she perched on the edge of the matching couch. "You don't have to do this. Especially not tonight."

"Lefty Shelton was my dad's cousin." She choked on his name.

"Maybe that's enough for tonight." Clay moved over beside her.

She leaned into his comforting arms. "My mother was a high school junior with plans to become an oncologist. Some friends invited her to the rodeo, and she met Lefty. They started dating, and she tried to convince him to get a real job, that the rodeo was too dangerous."

"Let me guess. He wouldn't give it up."

Rayna nodded. "They dated through the rest of high school and split up when she left for college. Daddy had loved her from afar through her entire relationship with Lefty. They started dating in college, got married, and only saw Lefty at family gatherings. Mom quit college after I was diagnosed with asthma because Daddy didn't trust anyone to take care of me, but he went on to med school. As time passed, tensions with Lefty eased, and my parents started going to the rodeo."

Clay handed her the water, and she took a quick sip.

"One night, Lefty fell and the bull charged. I was there, sitting in my mother's lap, feeling her terror. It's burned into my brain."

He held her tighter. "You don't have to tell me any more."

"Daddy got me and Adam out of the arena as quickly as he could." She trembled against him. "But my mother wouldn't go. She went to the hospital with Lefty. Daddy got someone to stay with us and went there to confront her. That's when she told him. They'd been having an affair."

Clay's arms tightened around her. "Musta broke his heart."

"She chose Lefty over us," Rayna whispered.

"And you didn't remember any of this until, in my brilliance, I insisted on taking you to the rodeo."

She pulled away to look at him. "It's not your fault. You had no way of knowing." She stood to pace.

Clay wore a disgusted scowl. "I brought this all back to haunt you. You'd have been fine if you'd never had the disadvantage of meeting me."

"Not necessarily. Brother Timothy said repressed memories strike at any time. Eventually it would have happened, and it didn't come at the first rodeo. I did have a slight asthma attack then, too, but I didn't remember anything until the last one."

"Why didn't you tell me the first time?"

"It wasn't as bad, and I didn't want you to think I couldn't handle the job."

Clay sighed and ran his fingers through his mussed curls. He stood and cut her off, midpace. "I've got big, willing shoulders. No matter what you say, I brought this on you."

"It's not your fault."

"Either way, let me help you deal with it."

Rayna blew out a shaky breath and melted into his comforting embrace. "My mom's back. And my dad's falling for her all over again. It's like he's forgotten everything she did to us. I can't. Neither can Adam. We can't even bring ourselves to go over there."

"Dear Lord, bring Rayna comfort and peace as only You can." Clay held her tighter.

Praying with the man she loved. What could be better? Except she couldn't love him. Love only set hearts up to crumble.

"Back when she left, Daddy told us she had to. That was the only explanation we got."

"You were too young to understand."

"I used to fantasize that she had some important thing

she had to do. That she went back to med school because she was the only one who could go to some foreign land and find a cure for kids with cancer. Or maybe she really died, and Daddy didn't want to tell us. That somehow she had no choice in leaving us."

"Here, lay down on the couch."

She complied, too emotionally exhausted to do much else.

He pulled a warm throw from the back of a chair and tucked her in, as he would a child. With a soft kiss pressed to her forehead, he crossed to the recliner facing her.

❧

Within minutes, Rayna's breathing slowed. Fast asleep. Exhausted.

Clay turned off the lights except for a lamp and brushed another kiss on her cheek. She didn't stir. He hated to think of her waking and reliving the evening alone. With heaviness in his chest, he left.

Her past held a doozy of a horror. How could she deal with the knowledge that her mother had chosen a man over her? A cowboy at that. No wonder a relationship with him gave her pause.

Clay climbed into his truck, fished his cell from his jacket pocket, and punched in the number. It rang twice.

"Dr. Landers here."

"It's Clay Warren. I just left Rayna's place, and I'm calling to let you know she's okay."

"The session went well?" Worry resonated in his tone.

"Yes, sir. Said she feels better than she has in years. She's asleep. Worn out. I hate for her to be alone, but she wouldn't let me bring her to your house."

"You're sure she's okay."

"Yes, sir." Clay started his truck. "I'm thinking I might stop by to see about her in the morning."

"Good idea. You do that, and have her call me."

❧

Persistent tapping. Rayna squinted. Sun streamed through the open curtains. *Why am I on the couch?* Fully dressed. Stiff, she sat up and stretched. Then it all came back.

"It's Clay, you all right?"

"I'm coming." She smoothed her hands through her hair. No use. She glanced in the mirror and groaned. At least the blotchy redness and swelling around her eyes were gone.

"Hey." He leaned against the door facing, looking like six million bucks. "I didn't want you to be alone this morning." He pulled her into his arms.

His thoughtfulness lodged a lump in her throat. *Oh God, please work things out between us. Help us to find a happy medium together. Work a miracle here. I don't want to lose this man.*

"I called your dad last night to let him know you were okay. He wants you to call him. Are you going to work today?"

"Yes. We have a meeting at ten o'clock to go over the final details of the ad campaign. Then it's on to the production company for more commercials."

"Are we still on for Saturday night?"

She nodded.

"I'll scoot and let you call your dad. He's worried." Clay tipped his hat.

"I really appreciate you. For everything you've done."

He winked and her heart skipped a beat.

❧

Clay wore his usual casual attire topped with a tuxedo jacket and looked good doing it.

"Are you sure this is okay for a Christmas party?" He parked at the upscale restaurant. "You're all sparkly."

"You look great." He might not fit her lifestyle, but even though she wore strappy high heels, he had a good inch on her. A definite plus, since she towered over so many men, and she hated to wear flats with a dress.

"So do you. You're gorgeous in black."

Reminding herself to stay seated, she waited until he came around the truck to open her door and give her a hand since she had heels on.

"Sure you don't want to go somewhere else? Just the two of us?"

"Clay, stop. I'm getting employee of the year."

Inside Morton's Steakhouse, she weaved her way through the throng into the dark-paneled private dining room. Occasionally, she stopped to introduce him.

"Rayna." Kendra and her ample cleavage cut them off. "Hey, want to sit at our table?" She motioned toward Gabby, Adam, and a man Rayna didn't know.

"Okay."

Kendra whispered in her ear. "I can't believe you brought the cowboy."

If you could've pulled it off, you'd have brought him.

Clay pulled out her chair.

"This is my date, Jake. This is Rayna Landers and Clay Warren. We recently wrapped up a huge ad campaign for Clay."

"What kind of party is this?" Jake huffed. "No alcohol."

"I warned you, babe." Kendra trailed her fingertips down his shoulder.

"My kind of party." Clay winked at Rayna.

"Mine, too." Rayna stashed her evening bag under her chair. "Actually, this is the first time Gabby and I have come in a few years."

"Yes, of course, the virgin twins don't drink." Kendra smirked.

Warmth enveloped Rayna from her head to her toes.

Adam cleared his throat. "Both admirable attributes. Last year at the party, a few people got out of control and the company considered canceling the whole thing, but Gabby started a petition to have an alcohol-free party."

"Yes, and I thought about not coming." Kendra rolled her eyes.

Clay surveyed the menu. "What? No barbecue?"

Rayna laughed as he leaned near her ear.

"What do you say we go out for coffee after this shindig?"

His whisper sent a delicious shiver over her.

Sitting across from Rayna in a corner booth at the coffee-house, Clay thought life couldn't get any better. Machines whooshed and steamed with a mouthwatering mix of aromas as the barista concocted their drinks. At the late hour, only a few other caffeine addicts occupied tables.

"Sorry you were bored tonight."

"I wasn't bored." He squeezed her hand. "How could I be bored with you?"

The barista brought their order.

Rayna tasted her frothy latte. "We'd barely arrived, and you were talking about leaving."

"I just wanted to be alone with you." He traced the back of her hand with his fingers. "What's with Kendra? Is she really your friend? You don't seem to have anything in common with her."

"We don't. Gabby and I are on a mission with her. Kendra isn't a Christian, so we're trying to witness to her."

"That's awesome. I'll pray you make headway." Clay sipped his Colombian blend. "Was it true, what she said about you?"

A pretty blush crept up her neck to wash over her face. "Yes."

"I'm glad." He intertwined his fingers with hers. "How about we spend the day together tomorrow? We'd start out with church then lunch at the ranch and horseback riding. Then evening church."

"Sounds nice."

"Have you talked to your dad this week?"

"A couple of times."

"I know you don't want to deal with your mom, but I don't think she's going away."

"What makes you think she'll stick around this time?" Her voice caught.

"Rayna?"

"Can we not talk about this?"

"People make mistakes. Maybe your mom realizes she made one in leaving. Give her a chance."

"I think her mistake was coming back. I can't let her hurt Daddy again."

"Your father seems like a reasonable man. He can take care of himself."

She sighed. "I'm tired of this wall between us. Daddy and I used to be so close."

"Then take the first step in scaling it. How about after lunch tomorrow, we visit your folks?"

"I'm willing to do anything to get my father back." She sipped her latte. "Even if it takes making nice with her."

"Maybe your relationship with your mom can be repaired."

"I doubt it, but I'll see if Adam can join us. I'm kind of worried about him. Since this whole thing came out, we haven't talked much."

"You both need to deal with things. Together." He brought her hand to his lips and brushed a kiss across her knuckles, relishing the shudder that moved over her. "And I'll be here to help any way I can."

❧

Clay pulled into the Landers's drive. The thick olive pullover, corduroy dress pants, and loafers felt weird. Like it wasn't his skin. With no hat, his curls flipped out every which way.

He caught Rayna staring as they walked to the house. "What?"

"You look a lot different."

"Good or bad?"

"Good."

"I clean up good, huh?" He winked. "I figured since the rodeo is a sore spot with your bunch, I'd drop the usual attire."

The door swung open and her mother forced a big hug on Rayna. "I was so glad you called."

Rayna's arms remained stiff at her sides.

"Name's Clay Warren, ma'am. Rayna and I—we, um— work together. Nice to officially meet you."

Mrs. Landers shook the hand he offered. "Thank you for bringing Rayna to see me."

Tension swirled through the room as Dr. Landers and

Adam brooded on the couch.

Rayna turned to Adam. "I'm glad you're here."

"It's nice to have the whole family together." Rayna's mother tried to keep things light.

"None of us but you ever went anywhere," Adam snapped.

Mrs. Landers's face crumpled. She clasped a hand to her mouth, spun away, and ran from the room.

"That's enough." Dr. Landers slammed a fist on the coffee table. "We're not here to hurt one another."

"That's all she's ever done." Adam stood. "I'm leaving."

Rayna followed her brother to the front door. "I'm sorry, Daddy, we just can't do this."

"I'll be right there, Rayna. You wait on me." Clay's jaw clenched as the door shut behind her. "Sir, if I may. My pastor helped Rayna deal with some of her feelings. Maybe he could help."

"I resent the insinuation. If my family needs any counseling, I'll take care of it."

Clay held his hands up. "Sir, I don't mean any disrespect, and I'm certainly not a professional. But. . ."

"But what?" Torment pinched Dr. Landers's expression.

Clay's heart dipped. "Have you ever thought maybe you're too emotionally involved to help set things straight?"

"What's that supposed to mean?" Dr. Landers paced the living room. "Who do you think you are nosing in our affairs? You're just a. . ."

"A cowboy. But when I was a boy, my dad lost. . ." *Don't mention any names.* "A real good friend, and it ate at his gut. He started seeing Brother Timothy and talked it all out. After that, he could deal with it. I'm thinking if talking helped my dad, maybe it could help your family."

The pacing slowed and Dr. Landers stopped at the window. "I fell for Dayle when Lefty introduced us, but I never let either of them know it. Then he hurt her. And I tried to pick up the pieces for her." He swallowed hard. "I'm not sure she ever really fell in love with me or if she just needed me."

"She loves you, sir. I could see it in her eyes."

He hung his head. "I failed her."

"Loving someone is never failure."

"Are you and Rayna involved?"

"I'd like to be, but she thinks she's got too many issues to be pondering a relationship. Especially with someone in my line of work. I'd better get her home."

Dr. Landers nodded. "Thanks for trying to help. I'll think about what you said."

Clay hurried to the truck and climbed in.

Rayna tried to stifle a yawn.

"I'm glad you waited. I was worried you might catch a ride with Adam."

"We bonded in our mutual rage."

"Doesn't sound healthy."

She rolled her eyes. "What were you doing in there?"

"Trying to talk your father into taking your whole family to see Brother Timothy." Clay started the engine. "Tell me something. Did you miss your mom when you were a kid?"

She turned toward the passenger's side window. "I longed for her. A feminine touch. Someone to put ribbons in my hair and give me perfumed hugs."

Clay took her hand in his. "Then look at this as a chance to make up for all that lost time."

"But what if"—her voice caught—"I forgive her and she leaves again?"

"Then you'll have done the right thing. And I'll be here for you to lean on."

❧

Warmth swept through Rayna as Clay took her hand in his and they stepped inside the church. Without her saying anything, he'd dressed casually in khakis, a turquoise shirt, and tennis shoes. No pearl buttons or hat. He looked uncomfortable and Rayna could have kissed him for his effort.

"I'll walk you to the office then wait in the sanctuary if you need me." Clay moved his hand up to tip his hat and met air.

A slow grin tugged at his mouth.

Again, Rayna wanted to kiss him. Just for looking so good. And for sticking with her—baggage and all.

They neared the office. Her parents waited in the lobby.

"Rayna, I'm so glad you agreed to come." Her mother patted her arm.

Rayna stiffened.

What should she call her mother? She didn't deserve to be called Mom. Dayle? The Adulteress? The Woman Who'd Ruined Their Lives?

Brother Timothy stepped out of his office. "Hello." He offered his hand. "I'm. . . Dayle Newcomb—is that you?"

The light of recognition dawned in her mother's eyes. "Timothy Andrews. Look at you—a preacher. I never would've guessed. Not in nine million years."

"Dayle and I went to high school together, but we ran in rather different crowds."

"I was the biggest flirt, but I didn't hang with the guys who only came out after midnight."

Rayna stifled a gasp. Who was her mother to judge anyone?

"Clay's well aware of my testimony." Unflustered, Brother Timothy grinned. "But Rayna's rather in the dark. You see, I didn't always live my life on the straight and narrow. Let's just say the Lord saved me, not only from the fires of hell, but from drugs and alcohol as well."

"Which gives you a more powerful testimony," Clay drawled.

"There's Adam. Daddy, why don't y'all start? Adam and I will be in shortly."

Mom updated the pastor on former classmates as Rayna stalked away.

As the office door closed behind them, Adam blocked her path. "We need to do this for Dad."

"I know." Rayna closed her eyes. "It can wait. Just let me take a few deep breaths. I want to talk to you."

Clay cleared his throat. "I'll be in the sanctuary."

Rayna waited until he was gone. "Why have you been so standoffish?"

"You didn't want to talk that first morning, so I gave you space."

She hugged him. "I don't need space. I need my brother back."

"You never lost me." He propped his chin on her head. "I remember more than you. I was six. I remember Lefty being around, playing with us. Then he disappeared the same time as our mother did. By my teens, I figured it out and asked Dad about it. I've been hiding the truth, trying to protect you for a long time."

"I'm okay. Especially if I have you." *And Clay.* "What changed your mind about Clay?"

"I figured you needed someone, and after getting to know him, I decided my childhood perspective of cowboys was skewed."

Rayna pulled away to look at him. "I'm not sure I can do this."

"Come on, sis." He slung his arm around her shoulder. "We promised Dad. We'll face it together."

❧

Clay looked at the clock in the sanctuary. The session had lasted longer than Rayna's. To the toes of his cowboy boots that weren't on his feet, he longed to be in there with her. The least he could do was be there when she came out. He hurried out into the lobby and plopped in a wingback chair.

The office door opened. Dr. Landers wore worry like a well-fitting saddle as he exited holding his ex-wife's hand. Rayna and Adam followed.

"We'd better go. It's getting late. I'll call tomorrow." Rayna pecked her father on the cheek and ignored her mother.

Dr. Landers's mouth tightened in a straight line, and he marched out the door, followed closely by Rayna's mom.

Rayna gave her brother a quick hug. "I'm so glad you came."

"Yeah." Adam's tone was dead. "See you tomorrow."

Clay waited until Adam's SUV pulled away and curled her into his shoulder as they walked to his truck. "What happened?"

"We aired all our dirty laundry, but nobody opened up. We kind of took sides—our parents against Adam and me."

They stopped at his truck, and he hugged her. "Maybe your folks are embarrassed since your mom knows Brother Timothy."

"She should be. I can't believe she had the nerve to say anything about his past."

"Brother Timothy's been very open about it, and your mother was only expressing shock at the change."

Rayna rolled her eyes. "We have another session next week after Christmas is over."

"Speaking of which, spend Christmas with me?"

"I'd love to, but Daddy's insisting we all gather at the house." She shook her head. "I just can't. Adam is joining Gabby's family, and she invited me, too. I already said I'd be there."

Forcing himself to let go of her, he opened the door, and she climbed in the truck.

"How about that evening?"

She smiled and his insides did a sideways bull twist. "I could probably manage to get away by then."

❧

Christmas night at Durlene and Ty's was a rowdy affair. Lacie and Mel arrived shortly after Rayna and Clay. The rustic home echoed the decorating style of the ranch with branding irons on the walls and rawhide curtain toppers. Twang was the order of the day—in music and speech.

Rayna missed her dad, but at least she and Adam were back to normal.

During the lively meal, talk of cattle, horses, and rodeos ruled. Clay did his best to include Rayna. Though surrounded by pleasant company, she obviously didn't fit in.

Afterward, she and Lacie helped Durlene clean the kitchen then went to the den to join the men.

"You okay?" Clay whispered.

Shivers pricked her skin as his breath ruffled the hair at her ear. "I feel. . ."

"Like a swan at a duck pond."

She laughed.

"Relax, everyone likes you. Especially me."

"It was the most enjoyable day I've had in a while." Warmth moved over her as he took her fingers in his.

"Let's go outside." Without waiting for an answer, he pulled her along to get their coats.

"It's cold. Why?"

"You'll see."

The evening air chilled her as they stepped outside.

Something made a rhythmic clacking against the driveway. A large shape neared in the moonlight. A single alabaster horse pulled a white hansom cab.

"Thanks for driving her over, Ben. How'd it go?"

"Come May, we're getting hitched." Ben climbed down from the cab.

"Congrats. I'll take it from here." He helped Rayna into the carriage then climbed in beside her and put his free arm around her shoulders. "Warm enough?"

Boiling. "I'm fine. Where did you get this?"

"It came with the ranch. I almost sold it awhile back, but I'm glad I didn't."

"You made poor Ben work tonight? How'd he get home?"

"He left his truck here, and I drove him over to the ranch so he could borrow the rig to propose to his girl." Clay pulled something from his pocket and held a ring box toward her. "Merry Christmas, pretty lady."

ten

Rayna gasped. Her heart revved. "If that's what I think it is, it's a bit soon. We've only known each other three months. Even if we have spent a lot of time together."

"Open it." His eyes shone in the lights lining the drive.

Slowly, she lifted the lid. Sparkling green gems winked at her. Earrings. Her insides quivered with a war between relief and disappointment. "They're beautiful."

"A real nice clerk at the jewelry store helped me pick them out. Said emeralds are always good for redheads. And I like you in green. 'Course, I like you in anything."

"They're real?"

"Of course. I wouldn't get my girl glass."

His girl. She closed her eyes and pushed the box toward him. "It's too much." She'd only gotten him three inspirational western novels.

"Worth every penny."

"But I didn't spend that much on you."

"Who's counting? I love the books. Give me something to do in between customers on the days it's my turn to work the desk at the ranch. I hate those days."

"A few months ago you were in financial straits. I can't accept these."

"My straits are fine since I did my time as a male model and won the world title. And I insist." He pushed the box back toward her then covered her hands with his. "Let's go for a ride. Yah."

The horse slowly clip-clopped along. Nestled against his side, she felt even warmer.

"Warm enough?"

Past boiling. "Yes."

His lips lowered to capture hers, and the fire moved all the

111

way down to her toes. Soft and gentle. And too short.

"Maybe next year, it'll be a ring," he mumbled.

❧

Rayna perched on the edge of the chair in Brother Timothy's office. He must be the most patient man on earth. Other than Clay.

"Do you remember Jackie Melton?" Her mother raised an eyebrow.

"Homecoming queen. Dated that football jock. What was his name?" The pastor snapped his fingers. "It's on the tip of my tongue."

"They called him Moose. Anyway, I ran into her awhile back. They got married and had four boys. Can you imagine four boys?" Dayle's expression clouded, and Daddy grabbed her hand. "I couldn't even stick around long enough to raise one."

Adam stood and stormed out, slamming the door.

Dayle's face crumpled.

Daddy hugged her while Brother Timothy knelt in prayer.

Rayna stood to follow her brother.

"I made such a mess of things." Her mother's soft whimpers tore at Rayna's soul. "I should have stayed and raised my babies. Lefty made so many promises, and I lost everything."

"I wasn't there for you like I should have been." Daddy closed his eyes. "I shouldn't have made you quit medical school. It was your dream."

"That was no reason to commit adultery. I never should have left. I should have come back. But I knew I wasn't worthy, and I knew y'all could never forgive me."

Rayna scurried out, scanning the lobby for Adam but finding only Clay. She made a nosedive for his shoulder.

"Adam left. I assured him I'd get you home."

"I think Lefty promised she could go back to medical school."

"Sounds like he was a real scallywag. Come on. Let's get you out of here. Think you've had enough for the night."

With his arm still around her, he turned her toward the door.

"Maybe he made it seem like her life was boring. Stuck at home with two kids, while his world was exciting, and he promised she could be a doctor. Her dream. It doesn't excuse what she did, but I can see her side."

"Good. I was hoping Brother Timothy could help." Clay opened the door for her then nestled her against his side as they continued to his truck.

"Before things got tense in there and Adam stormed out, Daddy suggested we all have breakfast together Sunday morning. I'm not sure we're ready for that."

"Just give it time."

&

After Clay left, Rayna couldn't sleep.

What do I do, Lord? How can I forgive her?

"I forgave those who nailed Me to the cross."

The phone rang. Almost ten o'clock. *Oh, don't let it be anything bad. Please.*

"Hello?"

"Just wanted to check on you," Clay drawled.

"I'm okay."

"You were so upset. I forgot to tell you that I'll be out of town a few days."

A chill settled in her chest. "Rodeo?"

"That, too. CWW signed me up for more commercials and three interviews on the radio. I'm gonna get it all done and be back at the Stockyards Friday night for the New Year's rodeo. It's the finals this year.

She'd actually forgotten about the campaign.

"I'd rather be with you, though. Nothing like kissing in the New Year with the woman who stole my heart. I've never had the pleasure before. Hate to miss out on it."

"Oh Clay, I'm still not sure about us."

"You don't feel the same way?" Hurt echoed in his words.

"You know I do. But we're still so different. The marriage thing doesn't seem so daunting." *Since I met you.* She closed her eyes. "But I'm still not sure about kids. You need someone who can share your dreams."

"I'm praying about it. God will work out the details for us. Get some sleep."

&

Rayna's office phone rang. An outside call. "Bradley & Associates. Rayna Landers speaking."

"How are you?"

Clay's voice filled her with renewed hope. "I've been treading water for the last twenty-two years and haven't sunk yet." She closed her eyes. "How's the publicity trail?"

"Lonely. Did I dream it, or did you say something last night about getting used to the marriage idea?"

"I've thought about it some. I might consider it if the right guy came along."

"The right guy, at your service. Keep praying. I love you, Rayna Landers."

Her breath caught. "And I love you, Clay Warren."

The line went dead, and she hung up.

In love with a cowboy. How did this happen? Well, if she was going to love a cowboy, she needed to make peace with the rodeo.

She hurried to Adam's office and tapped on his closed door.

"Come in."

"Hey, do you know where to get a ticket for the Saturday rodeo at the Stockyards?"

&

Rayna made her way through the crowded lobby into the arena. The stands were packed. Oh, for a glimpse of dark curls.

"Hey darlin'." His drawl set her heart aflutter, and his eyes sparkled. Chaps hugged his slim hips. An unwanted reminder of the bull waiting for him.

"Hey, yourself."

"I've missed you, gal."

"It's only been three days."

"I know, but I didn't like it. Let's not let it happen again. What are you doing here?" His arms came around her, and she felt like she'd made it home. His solid protective vest pressed against her heart. *Please keep him safe.*

"Came to see you, cowboy."

"Let's go somewhere to talk."

"I don't want to take your mind off the game."

"Too late for that."

She followed him out the back exit to a somewhat secluded alcove in the building.

"I'm thrilled to see you, but what are you doing here?"

"I figure I'm as comfortable at the rodeo as you are with photo shoots." She sighed. "If we're going to make this work, we both need to adapt."

"Let me get this straight. The last time you were here you had an asthma attack. So you just decided to stop by?"

"I like to take the bull by the horns. And with you, life includes bulls."

He cupped her face with tender hands. "You have no idea what it means to me that you're willing to do this. But I want you to go home. Now."

"No." Rayna shook her head.

"Please don't fight me on this." Clay's thumb traced her jawline. "I can't concentrate on what I gotta do if I'm worrying about you in the stands."

"You mean if I stay, you'll be distracted, and you might get hurt as a result?"

"That's exactly what I'm saying. Now, please. Go home."

She nodded. "Since you put it like that."

"I really appreciate you coming. A lot." He brushed his lips across her cheek then turned her toward a teenage cowboy. "Jeff, can you see the lady makes it to her car all right?"

Without a backward glance, she followed Jeff for several minutes before chancing a peek. Clay was gone.

She hesitated then turned back. "I forgot something."

The teenager shrugged then followed as she hurried toward the arena. She sucked in two quick puffs from her inhaler and found the first available seat, hoping Clay wouldn't spot her.

I can do this.

"Rayna."

She nearly jumped through herself.

Lacie's baby bulge was cutely covered in a sequined red blouse. "I thought I saw you with Clay. Why did he seat you over here? These are the worst seats in the house."

"He thinks I left."

"Why?"

"Clay doesn't want me here."

"Why did you come?"

"Because if things are going to progress between us—and I really want them to—I have to learn to love the rodeo along with the man."

"I see." Lacie tapped her chin with a scarlet fingernail.

"Will he see me if I sit here?"

"Probably not, but you won't see any of the action either. Maybe that's a good thing."

"How are you? How's Mel?"

"I'm waddling along. Mel's just the way I like him. Wonderful, perfect, and healthy. He had a bad ride last week, but no injuries. I pray and keep all of my fingers and toes crossed every time he goes out there."

Blond curls danced as she shook her head. "Us girls will never understand what it is about a bull that makes a man want to ride it. I quit trying to make sense of it years ago. You can't change a cowboy. You gotta take him for what he is and love him with all your might."

"How do you do it, Lacie? Spend year after year. . . What is it now, seven?" Lacie nodded and Rayna continued. "Seven years watching your husband—the man you love more than life itself—ride a creature that has the capability, motive, and drive to crush him."

"I love him." Lacie shrugged. "And he loves this."

Rayna could see enough. As events began, she cringed, hid her eyes, peeked through her fingers, and ducked her head. Despite the fidgets, she made it the entire night without her heartbeat multiplying or her breathing becoming minimized.

She even cheered when Clay won Stockyards Bull Riding Champ and Mel came in second.

When it was over, with Clay still in one piece, she ran to meet him. "Hey."

His eyes widened, and he scaled the fence. "What are you doing here? Tell me you sat in the car and just now came in."

"Sorry, I can't do that."

"Now Clay, Rayna was a real trooper tonight." Lacie patted her shoulder. "Nary a gasp, and she did it for you. Don't be too hard on her."

His arms came around her, and she gave herself over to the scent of dirt, sweat, and animal. With her head resting against his shoulder, it was paradise.

"What are we gonna do?" He propped his chin on the top of her head.

"Let God work out the details."

"Are you really okay?"

"I'm fine. The bronc and bull ride made me nervous, but I never got short of breath or anything like that."

"You can't come again."

"I will if you do."

"So that's how it is?"

"I won't hide from my fears." *Except where my mother is concerned.*

"Did you have to use your inhaler?"

"I used it in advance—just in case."

He pulled away and kicked a clod of dirt off his boot. Dust flew, and from the smell of things, it hadn't only been mud. A muscle in his jaw clenched. "That's why I don't want you here. I don't want you taking extra medication to deal with my livelihood. It would be better if you stay away from the bullpen."

"I can't."

"Why?"

"Because the man I love is in the bullpen."

With a heavy sigh, he looked heavenward then took her in his arms again.

"Ladies and Gentlemen."

Rayna jumped.

"Find that special one and hold on tight. It's almost midnight. Ten, nine, eight, seven, six, five, four, three, two, one."

Clay captured her chin and tilted her head back. His kiss was soft, tender, and held such promise. "I'm glad you stayed."

"Me, too."

ર

Rayna sat in the kitchen she'd grown up in, across the table from her mother. For the first time. That she could remember anyway. Adam sat beside her, and Daddy stood facing them at the island stove. Sausage sizzled and the spicy aroma made her stomach growl.

"I failed you both as a mother."

"I won't let you take all the blame, Dayle." Daddy pointed his spatula in their direction. "You never had a pattern to follow."

"True." Dayle closed her eyes. "My mother left when I was just a baby. I never thought I'd follow in her footsteps."

"I failed all of you," Daddy said. "I asked Dayle out when I knew she was on the rebound. I knew she didn't love me, but I thought if I could get her to marry me, she'd be mine."

"Nonsense, Nick. None of this is your fault." Dayle swiveled her chair toward him. "And I did love you. I still do. But I didn't realize what I had until it was too late."

"Then to top everything off, I made you quit school."

"I needed to be home with the kids."

"You saw your dream of being a doctor slipping away, while I pursued my degree. No wonder you resented me."

"Let's stop apologizing and blaming ourselves." Dayle turned back to the table. "Save this stuff for our therapy sessions. This family begins now. Now that I see the blessings I have."

"You mean the same blessings you threw away for Lefty Shelton?" Adam crossed his arms over his chest.

"That's enough Adam." Daddy rounded the island and

set a platter in the middle of the table with a thump hard enough to shatter the stoneware.

The golden omelets laden with green peppers, sausage, and cheese turned Rayna's stomach. "I've lost my appetite."

"Me, too." Adam stood and grabbed his jacket. "Besides, we don't want to be late for church."

"Maybe we could all go together." Dayle pushed her plate away. "That's what I wanted to tell y'all this morning. Your father and I went to see Brother Timothy last night. I accepted Jesus."

Daddy cleared his throat. "And your mother and I are planning to remarry."

Rayna gasped.

"Please." Daddy claimed a chair between Rayna and her mother. "Can't we have a nice breakfast and then go to church as a family? I think if Jesus can forgive your mother, the two of you can."

A chair scraped the floor and Adam rejoined them.

Rayna hung her head.

Daddy took their mother's hand. "Let's pray over our meal."

❧

Clay knocked on her condo door. With the season starting all over again, so would Rayna's anxiety. Did he really want another season? He'd traveled too much, missed too much church, and missed too much life lately. But one more world title and he'd have officially lived up to his father's legend.

Her door swung open. "The right guy, at your service."

She lunged into his arms. "I'm glad you're here."

"Me, too." He backed her inside, away from prying eyes, and shut the door. "But I have bad news."

"What?" She pulled away to look at him.

"I have to leave town in a couple of days. CWW set up several interviews and public appearances." Clay rolled his eyes. "At least it's not a modeling gig."

"I'll miss you." Her words were barely a whisper.

"Me, too." He plopped on her couch, feeling like country

in the middle of *Vogue* magazine. "Tell me how breakfast with the folks went."

She blew out a big breath. "Tempers flared. Accusations flew. My mother announced she got saved. Daddy announced they're getting married again, and we all went to church together. You'll never guess what the sermon was on—forgiveness."

"Wow. It's awesome about your mom's soul. Was your dad a Christian during their marriage?"

"No. He started taking us to church after she left us. I guess he didn't know where else to turn."

"I'm glad he turned to the right place. You know, most folks would be thrilled if their parents reunited."

"It's a lot to take in. I'm having a hard time putting it all in the past like Daddy has."

Clay patted his shoulder.

She laughed and took his cue, laying her head on the waiting shoulder.

He inhaled her flowery scent. "Play hooky with me tomorrow. Spend the day with me at the ranch."

"Sounds tempting. I haven't called in sick or taken a personal day in two years."

"Tell you what. You might want to spend the morning praying, or with your folks, or sleeping in. I'll expect you around noon. But if you need more time, let me know. I think right now, repairing your family needs to come first."

"You must be the perfect man."

"Except for the rodeo thing."

She shivered against him.

≥•

Rayna stood in the ranch hallway glaring at the picture of Lefty Shelton. Strong hands gripped her upper arms from behind. She jumped.

"Sorry. Didn't mean to sneak up on you." Ty steadied her.

She turned to face him.

"He was a good man in the beginning. The fast lifestyle, the women, the money—it all went to his head. I tried to witness to him, but he wasn't interested. When he died, I felt I'd failed him."

"If only we could force others to do what we want."

"If only." Ty patted her shoulder. "You get plenty to eat?"

"Too much. Durlene's taco soup warms the soul."

Clay stepped into the hall. "There you are. How 'bout watching me train a horse?"

She shivered. "A bronc?"

"Nope. Natalie bought a new mare, and I'm training her for barrels."

She's still lurking about? "Sure."

"You young folks, skedaddle." Ty jammed his hat on. "Have some fun."

Rayna slipped her coat on and followed Clay outside. The crisp late-January air burned her lungs as they walked to the arena. She perched atop the fence to watch him at work.

The white mare had a speckled shadow across her hindquarters. "What breed is she?"

"An Appaloosa."

Clay led the horse around the barrels in a tight cloverleaf formation.

"How does that help her learn to run barrels?"

"It gets her accustomed to the pattern. We're just getting started."

He clicked his tongue. "Good girl. That's it." His eyes shone as he was obviously doing what he loved. And it was safe.

"When do you plan to quit the rodeo and give the ranch your full attention?"

eleven

"Only when I get too old, busted up, and decrepit to ride."
Clay shot her a crooked grin.

"You can't be serious?"

"I'm *dead* serious."

His word emphasis sent a shiver over Rayna.

"Hey, I was just kidding. Busted up and decrepit really
aren't my style."

"It's not funny. You told me you only got into the rodeo to buy
this place. With the CWW campaign, you could quit now."

"To be honest, at the end of every season I'm tired and I
ask myself, is this it? But I'm not ready to quit just yet."

"Why?"

"Somewhere along the way, I fell in love with"—Clay closed
his eyes—"the sound of the crowd chanting my name before
a ride. The feel of the rope wound around my hand. The
knowledge that it's me or the bull. The rush of adrenaline and
the smell—"

"Of manure." Sarcasm dripped from her words.

His eyes opened and anger blazed in their green depths.
"You don't even try to understand."

"No, I don't. Because I still can't handle the marriage and
kids thing if I have to worry about whether you make it
home from the arena every weekend."

One eyebrow rose. "We're talking marriage *and* family
now?"

"At least I know why I never wanted those things."

"You were afraid you'd end up divorced like your folks."

"How did you know that?"

"Because I know you. I've watched you watch her. So
you've faced your fears, and you're up to the challenge of
living."

"Yes, but not with a bull rider."

"What happened to both of us adapting?"

"What if you die?" Her voice quivered. "Where does that leave me?"

"I could get hit by a truck anytime."

"Yes, but when you ride bulls, the odds are against you living to be an old man, and I'd very much like you to do that for me."

"I can probably count on one hand the cowboys who've been killed by bulls." Clay stopped the horse, gave her a sugar cube, and walked over to the fence. "Remember, I'm ten feet tall and bull proof." He moved in for a kiss.

She jumped down and backed away. "I won't stand around and watch you get yourself killed."

"I don't plan on getting killed, so there's nothing to worry about. How can I convince you that nothing's gonna happen to me?"

"By quitting the rodeo."

"I plan to. Eventually. Just not now." He sighed and gazed heavenward. "Why am I the only one who has to give up something?"

"I don't understand why you're so intent on holding on to this—hobby. Okay, it helped you pay for the ranch and keep your employees, but you don't need the money anymore."

The muscle in his jaw twitched. "It's not a hobby. I happen to love what I do."

"I don't."

The fence creaked as he vaulted over it. "We can work this out, can't we? Surely there's some compromise. I already told you, you don't need to come watch."

"Trust me, I've seen enough bull attacks to last me a lifetime."

"It's settled then. You stay away from the rodeo, and I'll do my best to avoid bull attacks." He tipped her chin up and kissed her.

As her resolve puddled at his feet, her cell phone vibrated. She pulled away. "I need to get that. Could be the office."

Clay blew out a sigh.

"It's supposed to be a workday, so I'm on call." She dug the phone from her pocket.

But it was Daddy.

"Hello?"

"Rayna, I have an important invitation." Her father sounded desperate, which meant it was about her mother.

"What is it?"

"We'd like to get remarried on our original wedding date, Valentine's Day, and we want you and Adam to be there. I know it's still a few weeks away. But I wanted to give you plenty of time to work it into your schedule."

She took several deep breaths. "I'll have to check my calendar. What if we can't make it?"

Silence on the other end. For a moment, she wondered if he'd hung up.

"Then I guess we'll get married without you." The line went dead.

She closed her eyes.

"What is it?"

"An invitation to my parents' wedding on Valentine's Day." She leaned the top of her head into his chest.

His arms came around her. "I'd be honored to be your escort."

Just like he supported her in everything. Why couldn't she bring herself to support him? Because supporting him meant keeping him in the bull's eye. And she couldn't lose him. She'd just found him.

❧

The early February breeze curled inside Clay's collar.

Lacie tapped her foot. "Hey, you guys ready?"

Clay scanned his loaded extended cab truck. "I think we've got everything we need for the trip."

Lacie always supported Mel.

How had Clay allowed himself to fall for a woman who hated his work? What was it about her—the woman who wanted none of the things he did? Her vulnerability? Her wounded soul? She brought out the protector in him. Made him want to make sure she never got hurt again. Yet his profession made her hurt every weekend.

"What's wrong, cowboy? You look like your favorite horse died."

"Girl trouble." Mel clapped him on the back.

"Rayna asked me to quit the rodeo."

Lacie closed her eyes. "And you blew up?"

"Not exactly, but it's like there's been a big Brahma standing between us ever since, and we try to ignore it."

"What now?"

"I don't know."

"Clay Warren." Lacie pointed a red fingernail in his face. "Rayna's a great girl, but if you're gonna be safe tonight, you need to concentrate on the bull. I'll pray about the city girl for you."

ᐒ

The insistent knocking sent Rayna scurrying to the peephole. Daddy and Adam. She opened her condo door.

Daddy's shoulders slumped as he stepped inside, followed by Adam, who was holding a shoe box.

"What's wrong?"

"What's wrong?" Daddy's eyebrows rose. He shut the door behind him. "The woman I've loved all of my adult life is back. She's a Christian. She wants to marry me. She wants to be a mother to the two of you. She wants to make up for lost time, and you won't let her."

"Whoa." Rayna splayed her hands as if to ward off a blow. "She's the one who left—for some cowboy, and you expect us to just forget that?"

Daddy's throat convulsed. "She left me, too. But that's behind us now. This is our chance to start over. For all of us."

Rayna looked to Adam for backup.

He stood there, holding his box, mouth clamped shut.

"Can you help me out here, bro?"

"Mom and I had a good talk last night. We made peace."

Her eyes widened. "Mom?" *You mean the cowboy-chasing*

hussy who abandoned us?

"Let me talk to her." Adam steered Daddy toward the door. "I should have come alone."

"Watch the tapes, Rayna. I want our family back together. That's all I've ever wanted." Daddy looked sadder than she'd ever seen him. "For all of us to be together."

The door closed behind him with a thud.

She turned on Adam. "How did she brainwash you?"

Adam let out a big sigh. "Sit down and close your eyes."

"Why?"

"It might help you keep an open mind."

Unconvinced, she sat down in her favorite chair and closed her eyes.

"Mom's mother left when she was two. Her dad paraded different women in and out of her life until he died of cancer when she was fifteen. She went to live with her divorced grandmother, her only family, who encouraged her to dream of being a doctor and helped her through college."

The image of a lonely little girl came to life in Rayna's mind.

"She never stepped foot in church until she went with us to see Brother Timothy. She was never around younger kids. Though her grandmother was good to her, she wasn't a very demonstrative woman. She never hugged Mom. She encouraged her to be a doctor so that someday when she ended up alone, she'd be able to take care of herself."

Rayna opened her eyes. "She was following the only pattern she knew, but that doesn't make it okay."

"No, it doesn't. But she'd wanted to be a doctor for years. She was in med school, on task for her dream, when I was born. Then another baby."

"Who became an asthmatic toddler, and Daddy made her quit med school."

"She spent her days changing diapers and wiping runny noses while Dad went to school and got his master's degree."

"Okay, that would frustrate me, but that's what you sign on for when you get married." Yet she'd asked Clay to give up his dream.

"But in her family, if things weren't going well, someone left. Then add to the mix her high school sweetheart. He pushed her buttons with a med-school-shaped moon. Do you have a VCR?"

Rayna frowned. "It plays both. Why?"

He opened the lid of his shoe box and pulled out a video cassette. "I want you to watch these. I'll stay and watch them with you, or I'll go. Whichever you want."

She blew out a big sigh. "I want you to stay."

Adam slid a tape in and nabbed the control then sat on the sofa and patted the seat beside him.

Rayna moved over next to him.

The tracking was off and static filled the screen but eventually cleared. Dad hoisted Adam, maybe five at the time, on his shoulders. Mom chased after them with a cheery smile on her face and two-year-old Rayna in her arms. Daddy knelt and bucked a giggling Adam off onto a bed. Mom dove into the middle of the fray, laughing and kissing Rayna, Adam, and Daddy.

"Who filmed this?" *Lefty?*

"Mom's grandmother. A couple of times you can hear her harrumphing over all the love and happiness."

&

Rayna knocked and rang the bell. No answer. She let herself into her childhood home. "Hey, is anybody here?"

No answer. She made her way through the living room to the kitchen. Outside on the patio, she could see her parents dancing. Dancing. Her mother's smile lit the world. The same smile captured in the videos.

Rayna turned away to leave them in peace, but Daddy saw her and waved her out.

"Rayna, I'm so glad you came over." Mom twirled in Daddy's arms. "We've been taking waltz lessons. I've always wanted to waltz with the man I love. Isn't it lovely? We didn't get to waltz at our first wedding, but we will at our second."

"You've definitely gotten the hang of it."

"I'll make myself scarce." Daddy kissed her cheek as he

passed and whispered, "I'll trust you to treat your mother with respect."

For the first time since Rayna could remember, he whistled a tune as he left the room.

"He loves you."

"Yes. He's a wonderful man."

"I thought you came back because Lefty died, but he died years ago."

"He left me six months after I left you. For a groupie."

"Why didn't you come back then?"

"I didn't figure your daddy would have me. And he probably wouldn't have at that time. I hurt him so badly." Mom's voice broke. "I didn't want to leave with Lefty, but your father couldn't live with what I'd done. I had nowhere else to go."

"You didn't choose Lefty over us?" Rayna perched on the couch.

"Not intentionally." Mom sat beside her. "But after Lefty, your father couldn't trust me. If he would have let me stay, I would have. And I'd learned my lesson. I wouldn't have been unfaithful again."

"Daddy made you leave?"

"Don't be angry with him. In his eyes, I chose Lefty when I started our affair."

"Did Lefty kill himself?"

"Who knows?" Mom shook her head. "A one-car accident with a brick wall. He'd certainly made a mess of his life. He cheated on me. He cheated on the women after me, and he drank heavily, but maybe it was his time. Everyone has a time to die." Mom's eyes watered.

"Where did you go after he left you?"

"Back to my grandmother's. I finished medical school and became an oncologist like I always wanted. But it was empty without the three people I really loved. I never even dated again. Instead, I built my life around my career."

"What made you come back?"

"Breast cancer. The cancer doctor came down with it."

Rayna's breath stalled. "You're sick?"

"No. I beat it—last year. But during all the treatments and surgeries, I told myself if I lived"—her voice cracked—"I'd come home and beg for the rest of my living days until your father, Adam, and you could find it in your hearts to forgive me."

"I'm glad you're okay." A lump lodged in Rayna's throat.

Despite the moisture in her mother's eyes, a smile curved her lips.

Rayna leaned her head against her mom's.

A strong hand gripped Rayna's shoulder. "Looks like everything's okay here." Daddy wrapped them both in a hug from behind the couch.

"If you don't mind," Rayna whispered, "I'd like to come to your wedding."

❧

Valentine's Day afternoon, pre-ceremony, Rayna sipped her coffee and gazed out the kitchen window at the jungle of tulle and lace in the backyard.

"Rayna, what is with you? You're jumpier than I am." Mom was a vision in a creamy lace suit. "You're okay with the wedding, aren't you?"

"Definitely."

"Is it Clay? Why has he hung out with your dad and Adam today instead of with you?" Mom hugged her.

"He's here to support me." Rayna sighed. "But we're kind of at a crossroads. I brought up a taboo subject."

"You asked him to quit? I bet he took that well."

"Kind of like when Daddy asked you to quit med school."

Mom stood and moved to the window. "Do you go with him to the rodeos?"

"Once I started caring about him, it made me so nervous. Lately, I've tried not to go, but that makes me even more nervous because I don't know what's happening. I think I've been more miserable not knowing."

"You love this man, sweetie. And he's worthy of you. From what I've seen, you and Clay could have a lifetime of love.

Try to support him in everything, the way he does you."

The way Daddy should have supported his wife. "I guess I'm going to Fort Worth this weekend then."

"Your father told me about the asthma attack. Take your inhaler."

Rayna squared her shoulders. "I'll be okay."

"Preacher's here," Adam hollered.

"Oh, it's about time." Mom jumped up. "Let's get this show on the road."

Rayna hurried to the living room. Clay had gone all out and wore a complete suit. Not a trace of cowboy left, except for the crooked grin he shot her. Supporting her in everything. She closed the gulf between them and kissed his cheek.

ꙥ

Rayna shielded her eyes from the glaring lights of the arena to search for a seat. The place was packed. Maybe she could blend in with the crowd.

"Rayna, you're here?" Lacie sounded surprised.

"I couldn't seem to stay away."

The blond hugged her, protruding belly in the way. "I know exactly how you feel. Does Clay know you're here?"

"No. He'll worry about me, and I want him to worry about the bull instead. I'll stick around afterward. How much longer do you have to go?"

The announcer's voice came over the speakers, hawking the calf roping.

"Three months." Lacie rubbed a hand over her stomach. "Let's go to the lobby."

"I don't want Clay to see me."

"He won't in this throng."

In the lobby, the usual women stood in a circle. Rayna met a few new faces since some of the cowboys had changed girlfriends.

"I'm surprised to see you." Natalie offered a victorious smile. "You haven't been around lately, so I thought you and Clay were off."

"I was at his ranch the other day." Rayna forced a bright tone. "Your Appaloosa is beautiful."

"Yes, she is. I was there yesterday. Clay and I worked with her together."

"Clay and Rayna are still very much on," Lacie said. "They're too much in love to be off."

Put firmly in her place, Natalie backed down and didn't stay much longer.

"Don't let her bother you," Lacie whispered. "She's two-timing her Clay delusions anyway. There's a new bullfighter here, and Natalie has her sights set on him."

When the announcer's voice boomed again, she learned Clay would ride first in the lineup. At least it would be over soon.

Rage. Such an oh-so-fitting name for the enormous rust-colored creature as it exploded from the chute. Rayna cringed, peeking through her fingers to watch helplessly as the bull flung Clay from side to side like a rag doll. It was apparent right from the start: the bull was in control. In a short time, she'd learned what a good ride looked like, and this wasn't it.

Clay managed to stay on until the buzzer sounded, but Rage raged until her cowboy fell. He lay still, motionless.

Rayna screamed.

The beast charged toward Clay.

twelve

The bullfighter headed the furious creature off. Both bullfighters and the barrel man helped the pick-up man get Rage out of the arena.

Paramedics and cowboys surrounded Clay.

Tears streamed down Rayna's face. Lacie spoke to her, but she couldn't make sense of anything other than how still Clay was. Finally, her friend grabbed her hand and pulled her down the stands. Pandemonium broke out as a crowd moved toward the arena for a closer look.

"Suck on that inhaler thingy," Lacie instructed.

Rayna took two quick puffs, and Lacie dragged her out the back exit where an ambulance waited. "We'll find out where they're taking him, and I'll drive you to the hospital."

From the looks of him, the morgue would be more like it. Everything started to go black, and she leaned against a wall until her vision cleared.

An eternity later they carried Clay out on a gurney and carefully loaded him into the ambulance. Pale, unmoving.

Lacie launched toward one of the medics. "What hospital?"

Sirens wailed with a blur of spinning red lights. The horrifying race after the ambulance was the worst nine minutes of Rayna's life as she prayed harder than ever before. Even after arrival, the wait seemed to stretch into eternity when doctors wouldn't let her see Clay because she wasn't family.

Mel arrived, followed closely by Durlene and Ty.

No one spoke. While Mel and Lacie sat with Durlene and Rayna, Ty paced.

The last few weeks had been tense between them. They'd gone through the motions of conversation. *To hear his voice one more time.*

Double doors opened, and the doctor emerged.

Rayna's insides twisted.

"He's conscious. We'll keep him overnight to monitor the concussion, but he'll be fine. Might have to miss a couple of rodeos with that dislocated shoulder."

Durlene's relieved whoop echoed through the room.

Dropping to her knees, Rayna mumbled, "Thank You, God."

&

Rayna hesitantly entered the open door to Clay's hospital room. Morning sun streamed through the window. His exhausted parents sat on either side of him.

"Oh Rayna, you're here." Durlene perked up.

"Is everything all right?"

"Yes, but Ty and I need to head to the ranch. We're booked solid, and Mel and Lacie are working themselves silly."

"You two go. I came for the day."

"Good. I hate leaving him alone. I don't want him to wake up to an empty room."

"Has he been awake?"

"Off and on. Didn't sleep much, and he was disoriented." Ty shrugged. "Doc says he'll have to stay another day."

They both hugged her then left.

Claiming the chair by Clay, she leaned her head on his bed.

He moaned.

She straightened and took his hand in hers.

His eyelids fluttered.

Holding down the call button, Rayna watched as gorgeous green eyes opened and tried to focus on her.

"Hey." She kept her tone even, but tears welled.

"You're here?" His voice was weak, eyes watery.

"How do you feel?"

"Hurt."

"Where?"

"All over."

The door opened and a nurse entered. "How long has he been awake?"

"When he started coming around, I hit the call button. He said he hurts all over."

"I bet he does. Can you tell me your name, sir?"

"Clay Warren."

"Do you know where you are?"

He blinked then studied his surroundings. "Don't know which one but a hospital."

"Do you remember what happened, Mr. Warren?"

"I was riding a bull, but not very well."

"Yes sir, you were lucky. You're more lucid today. I'll go call the doctor." The nurse hurried out.

"Glad you're here. How did I do the other night?"

"You took second."

"Amazing. That was one bad ride."

"Yeah, but according to your dad, everybody had bad rides that night. Except Mel. He won."

"That's good." Another moan followed his words. "My shoulder's killing me."

"It's dislocated."

"Oh yeah. What a fine time for this. How are my standings?"

"Speak my language."

"Was second enough to qualify me for the world title?"

"You already won the world. Remember?"

"Oh yeah."

Tears singed her eyes. Rayna laid her cheek against his.

"Hey, I'm all in one piece. Just sore and a bit confused."

"That bull wanted to kill you, Clay. And it would've. The bullfighter got it turned away at the very last second."

"That's what bullfighters are for. And I'm fine. Ten foot tall and bull proof."

"I'll never forget you lying there, so still, and that horrible creature charging you."

"I wish you hadn't seen that, darlin'. Really, I do. But I'm fine. What were you doing there anyway?"

"I couldn't stay away."

"I guess we're even then. You didn't stay away, and I didn't avoid a bull attack."

ঌ

Rayna packed his things while Clay impatiently waited for his release papers. Thirty-six hours in the hospital was way too much downtime. At the doctor's strict orders to stay out of the rodeo for three weeks, he'd heard her sigh of relief.

He was already chomping at the bit. No way could he miss that much and stay in the lead.

"You out of here, cowboy?" The graying nurse poked her head in the door.

"It's supposed to be today, but at this rate, who knows. This is my fiancée, Rayna."

Shock registered in Rayna's eyes.

"Nice to meet you, ma'am. He'll be just fine. Now you take care of yourself, Mr. Warren."

"Thank you," Rayna called after her.

"I realize I haven't officially asked you to marry me. I'm waiting till I recover fully so I can get down on one knee and do it proper."

The door burst open, and Natalie lunged into Clay's arms. "Whoa, easy now."

"Oh Clay, I've been so worried about you."

So worried you waited two days before visiting. "Please be careful, Natalie. He's still healing."

Natalie turned on Rayna. "I would never hurt Clay."

"Not intentionally, I know, Nat, but I'm really sore."

The brunette perched on the bed and grabbed his hand. "Oh my poor baby," she cooed. "What can Nat do for you?"

Rayna rolled her eyes. "Actually, I'm going home in a bit," Clay said. "Why don't you and Rayna walk out together? She was just going to move her car around."

"I would've come sooner, but I hated to see you hurt." Her full lips dipped into a pout, and she moved in for a kiss.

He turned his cheek to her.

Disappointment registered in her eyes. "Glad you're better. I can see myself out."

The door closed behind her, and Rayna turned to him. "Thanks for trying to stick me with your groupie-wannabe."

"You know there's never been nothin' between us. Right?"

"Only in her dreams."

"I guess Lacie filled you in on her. Lord knows I've never encouraged her. Sorry I tried to saddle you with her, but I'm too tired to keep her at bay."

"It's a wonder she didn't take the offer just to get me away from you."

"Seems like she'd give up after a while."

"You're a hard guy to give up on."

"I'm glad you feel that way."

Her eyes held that guarded look. Holding something back. Hesitant to get too close, like she wasn't planning to stay. *How do I keep her, Lord? Without giving up a big chunk of myself?*

⁂

Durlene ushered Rayna up the ranch house stairs and knocked on Clay's door.

"Come in."

"His room's right through there."

Leaving the door open, Rayna hesitated. She'd never even been to his suite, much less in his bedroom. The decor was much like the downstairs. Cowboy couture.

"Rayna, is that you?"

She stepped through the doorway.

He sat propped up with numerous pillows, looking more rested after sleeping in his own king-size bed.

"You look beautiful. A sight for sore eyes. A sore noggin. A sore shoulder. Not to mention numerous other sore spots."

Gently, she kissed his cheek and sat in the chair beside him.

"Come sit by me." He patted the bed.

"I don't want to hurt you."

"You won't. This is my good side. Come on. I wanna hold you. The door's wide open, and I'm in no shape to try anything. Besides, have I ever?"

Moving to the bed, she ever so gently leaned into him. Oh

the feel of being nestled against his side. She could stay here forever.

"I'm going to the Stockyards next weekend. Wanna come?"

"I'll breathe easier with you sitting beside me."

"But I won't be. Sitting beside you, I mean."

"Clay." Her voice trembled. "Please don't tell me. You don't plan to ride again so soon. Do you?"

"I can't afford to miss. I have to stay in the top five to get a chance at the title again."

She pushed away from him and stood. "But the doctor said no rodeo for three weeks. And you've got all season."

"The more bulls I ride the better. Doc says he can tape me up good as new."

"Who?"

"The rodeo doctor."

She stood and stalked back and forth across the small room. "You plan to ride a bull again next weekend?"

"It's what I do."

Red-hot fire coursed through her veins, and she whirled toward him. "A bull put you in that bed."

"Listen, sweetheart, I learned a lot this time. Dad made me watch the tape a zillion times last night. I know what went wrong. Don't worry."

"This time? I can't believe you want to ride one of those. . . beasts, maybe even the same one that tried to kill you."

"It's a concussion and a dislocated shoulder. That's all."

"You didn't see the murderous look in that bull's eyes. I did, and I don't want to see it again."

"Let's get married."

Tears filled her eyes and no words came. The bed creaked, and she felt him standing behind her. She turned to face him. He pulled her into his arms. She savored the embrace—the feel of him one last time—then pulled away.

"If you go back to the rodeo, I won't be there."

Clay frowned. "So that's it?"

"That's it—the rodeo or me." If not for the pain in her chest, the words would sound comical. But it wasn't funny, only heartbreakingly serious.

"Well then." Anger hardened his handsome features. "Maybe I'll see you around."

Head held high, she stalked out of his room and downstairs. Thankfully, she didn't run into either one of his parents.

She hurried to her car and started the engine. Taking deep, slow breaths, she turned onto the highway.

Her vision blurred. A mile down the road, she had to pull over.

❧

"Rayna, I hope you'll join us for supper," Mama called from the hall.

Clay wiped his eyes.

Mama stepped in the doorway. "Did she leave already? Oh doll baby, what's wrong?" She knelt beside his bed.

"She's gone, Mama."

"No, that girl loves you. You'll work it out."

"She gave me an ultimatum."

"Her or the rodeo? And you picked the rodeo."

He nodded. It didn't make much sense. Choosing a bull over the beautiful Christian girl he loved. But if he gave up the rodeo now—because she wanted him to—they'd both be miserable. But. . .more miserable than now?

Footsteps sounded in the hall. Clay looked up.

Mel filled the doorway. "Hey, everything all right in here?"

Clay swiped his tears. "Sure. What's up? Where's Lacie?"

"Downstairs. Her ankles have been swelling, so I put her in that big recliner, made sure her feet were up."

"I'll go see about her." Mom patted Clay's leg.

Though the light in Mel's eyes remained bright, the lines around his mouth seemed strained. "There's something I need to tell you."

Sounded serious. "What? Is it twins?"

"I'm retiring. After this season—win or lose."

Clay swallowed hard. "You okay with that?"

Mel nodded. "I've been praying about it. It's the right

thing. Sometimes you gotta do what's right for the woman you love. And I'm tired. If I could rodeo every Friday and Saturday night at the Stockyards like we used to before we made it big, I might stay. But we've hit the big time. We're expected to make the Cinch finale again. My heart's just not in it anymore."

"Did she ask you to quit?"

"Nope." Mel settled into the chair beside Clay. "I've been trying to talk her into starting a family for over five years, but I thought she wasn't interested. We finally hashed it out back in October. By then, she was already two months along, and I learned she wanted kids as much as I do. But she was afraid something might happen and she'd be left to raise our children alone. She's more important than the rodeo, and I don't want to be on the road while my kid grows up without me."

"I'm really happy for you." Clay swallowed the lump in his throat. "It won't be right competing without you next year."

"Maybe you'll win more." Mel slapped him on the back, thankfully on his good side.

❧

Rayna worked even more hours, hoping to forget.

Clay was decidedly back in the saddle. Over the last few weeks, Rayna caught glimpses of him on television. Despite dislocating his shoulder again during a rough ride, Clay was determined to make it to the Cinch Series finale again.

His print ads were in every magazine she happened to thumb through, and her television seemed to only play his commercials. By early March, she'd stopped turning it on.

Instead she stared at his ad on her computer at work. She pulled it up at least once a day. Just to torture herself.

"Hey, you okay?" Gabby stood in the doorway with Adam. The concern in her voice didn't touch the light in her eyes.

"Sure." Rayna closed the ad. "You two look ecstatic."

"Look!" Gabby surged forward, holding out her left hand. A sparkling diamond graced her ring finger. "Can you believe it? He gave it to me at lunch."

Rayna gasped. "That's awesome."

Gabby twirled across the office. "I kind of had a thing for Adam from the moment I saw him."

"You did?" Adam's brow rose. "Why didn't you tell me?"

"I was waiting, and waiting, and waiting for you to notice me." Gabby kissed his cheek.

Rayna hugged her. "I've never seen you so happy. Have you set a date?"

"April tenth. That only gives me a month to get everything together, but I've been waiting for Adam my whole life. Why wait any longer? Will you be my maid of honor?"

"Of course I will. Please don't make me wear a stupid-looking dress."

"It's tradition. Organza froufrou. See you later. I won't get any work done today." Gabby kissed Adam's cheek again and bounced out the door.

"Congrats." Rayna hugged him. "Sorry. I've been rather self-absorbed."

"I would say distracted."

"Just because my romance fell apart doesn't mean I can't be happy for you. In fact, I'm thrilled."

He grinned. "Me, too."

"If only you two had listened to me sooner, you could have been this happy all along. Just say it—Rayna was right."

"This time—Rayna was right." Adam laughed and turned toward his office.

❧

Sunday morning, Rayna stood at her closet door trying to decide what to wear to church. Her phone rang. "Hello?"

"It's Durlene Warren." Clay's mother didn't sound her usual happy-go-lucky self.

A chill skittered up Rayna's spine.

thirteen

"What's wrong?" Rayna's heart pounded. "Is Clay all right?"

"Physically, yes."

Squeezing her eyes shut, she blew out a big breath.

"But Mel Gentry died at the rodeo last night."

She gasped. Nausea turned her stomach.

"Where is Clay?"

"At the ranch."

"I'll be right there." She dressed quickly, grabbed her purse, and hurried to her car.

The city girl had stayed away from the cowboy and the rodeo for almost a month, but now he needed her. Not to mention poor Lacie, whose worst nightmare had come true.

Rayna trembled. Without a doubt, she knew Clay and Lacie had both witnessed Mel's death.

She hadn't known him long or even well, yet her hands shook. Pressure welled in her chest and lodged a lump in her throat. Poor Clay, Lacie, and Mel's fatherless child.

Durlene and Ty met her at the door. "Oh Rayna. I'm so glad you came. He's in his suite. He needs you."

She followed Ty up the stairs.

"Son, there's someone here to see you." Ty stopped halfway up. "Your mama's making some herb tea. Tastes like the dickens, but it'll help settle frayed nerves. I'll bring it up in a bit." He motioned Rayna ahead. "Thanks for coming."

Clay sat facedown at his kitchen table, his back toward her.

Maybe she shouldn't have come. They hadn't parted on good terms. At such a horrible time in his life, she might be the last person he wanted to see. But it was too late.

He turned to her. Shock registered in his eyes. He stood, broken, shoulders sagged, and took a step toward her.

Relieved, she closed the gap between them. This time, she

provided comfort. Or tried to, as his sorrow soaked her silk blouse. "I'm so sorry."

"It wasn't even a bull," he mumbled. "A bronc and not even one of the wilder ones."

"Come sit down. How's your shoulder?"

"Better. Mel was planning to quit after this season." He settled on a tall bar stool.

She claimed the one by him. "Where is Lacie? How is she?"

"A wreck. Her parents are there. I should be there."

"Not like this."

"Don't guess I'd be much use to anybody." He leaned forward, facedown on the breakfast bar. "I held it together for her last night, but today it's hitting me full force."

"I honestly don't know what to say."

"You being here helps—more than you'll ever know."

She rubbed the tensed muscles along the back of his neck then shifted off the stool to embrace him.

He shuddered, and his tears soaked her shoulder again.

☙

The next day, Rayna knocked on the door of the ranch-style house with the bright turquoise door while Clay held the bowl of chicken soup she'd made.

A woman answered. A dark-haired carbon copy of Lacie.

"Hi, Star, how is she?"

"Not good. How 'bout you?"

Clay shook his head. "This is Rayna. She and Lacie sat through a few rodeos together."

"Nice to meet you." Star's hand trembled as she clasped Rayna's. "I'm Lacie's older sister. Come on in. She's in her room. Won't come out. Mama and Daddy are with her."

Rayna gestured toward the bowl Clay held. "If she's sleeping, we can leave the soup and come another time."

"Trust me. She's not sleeping." Star ushered them to the kitchen decorated with sage and copper roosters. Clay set the pot in line with the others on the marbleized counter.

"Do you think I should stay here?" Rayna whispered.

"She'll be glad to see you. She's always liked you and prayed we could work things out."

Their gaze held for a moment.

Star led them down the hall lined by Mel's rodeo photos.

Curled in a ball on the bed, Lacie pressed a pillow against her bulging stomach. Her parents hovered nearby.

Rayna hesitated in the doorway. Should she even be here? She didn't know Lacie well, but Clay had wanted her to come. Now she felt like an intruder.

"Lacie, Clay's here," her mother cooed.

Blue eyes opened. "I don't have any more tears."

Clay sat beside her. "Me neither."

"I'm glad you came."

"We'll be close, sugar." Her dad patted her arm.

"I think I'll go, too." Rayna turned away.

"Rayna." Lacie sat up and reached for her hand. "Don't go. He was gonna quit. At the end of this season."

"He loved you very much."

"Clay, would he have been happy? Without the rodeo?"

"Yes." He stroked her tangled blond hair.

"I keep worrying he might not have wanted to quit. Maybe he was distracted. Maybe that's what caused—"

"No. He was looking forward to a new phase in his life. He was at peace with being a husband and father."

"I wish he'd gotten the chance." She clasped her swollen abdomen. "Now this little fella won't know his daddy."

Despite her earlier claim, Lacie's tears spilled.

Clay gathered her in his arms.

⁂

On the way back to the ranch, Clay glanced at Rayna. Her profile was unreadable. He still couldn't believe she was there. More than anything, he wanted to lay his head in her lap and bawl like a baby.

Instead, he tried to clear his head, to put scattered thoughts in order. *Don't say the wrong thing.* "I'm glad you're here."

She didn't respond.

"Why'd you come?" *Smooth.*

"You asked me to."

"No. I mean to the ranch yesterday. When you heard about Mel, why'd you come?"

"Because I knew you were hurting. I wanted to help."

Okay, she still cares. "What does this mean for us?"

"I don't know."

"Come on, Rayna. Don't make me pull it outta you."

"I honestly don't know. I'm here because you lost your best friend. You've helped me through some rough patches. Now I'm here for you. And Lacie. After the funeral, I don't know."

"Fair enough, I guess."

"Would you rather I leave?"

"No." He reached for her hand.

She entwined her fingers with his. "Let's just get through the next few days. Is the baby a boy?"

"Little booger's always turned so they can't tell. Guess Lacie's hoping for a boy. It's not fair."

"No, it's not."

"Mel had so much to live for." His vision blurred. "Everything they wanted was within grasp. Now. . .he's gone."

"Clay, pull over. You're in no shape to drive."

With tears dripping from his chin, he slowed then eased onto the shoulder of the two-lane highway. Rayna put her arms around him as sobs racked his soul.

"I mean, I know it was his time." With his chin resting on top of her head, Clay relished the feel of her comfort. "If he hadn't been at the rodeo, it could've been a car wreck. If he'd have stayed home all day, the roof would've fallen in. It was his time. I just wish it hadn't been."

"I also think God gives us good sense. And if we don't use it, we might run out of time sooner than He planned."

He pulled away to look at her. "You really believe that?"

"Yes."

"You know, there comes a point when you have to give it all to God. He's big enough to protect us. From a horse, or a bull, or our own stupidity." He cupped her silky cheek in his hand. "I love you, and I really need you right now. I need to know you're here for the long haul."

She swallowed hard.

Clay pulled her into his arms. Grief welled in his chest. For Mel. For Lacie. For their unborn child. And for the woman he couldn't have. As soon as the funeral was over, Rayna would walk out of his life. Again.

ॐ

That evening, Rayna left the ranch house just behind Brother Timothy and his wife. "Brother Timothy, could I speak with you for a moment?"

"Of course."

"Take your time. I'll be in the car." Joan left them alone.

"Something on your mind?"

She hesitated. "It seems silly to bother you with something so trivial."

"Nothing is unimportant to God. Here, let's sit down." He ushered her to a well-lit redwood picnic table.

"I'm in love with a bull rider."

"And Clay is in love with you." Brother Timothy frowned. "Both Christians. The perfect match, but the rodeo is a nightmare for you."

"We broke up, and I've been miserable."

"He has, too."

"Mel's death reiterates all the reasons we can't be together. I'm trying to be here as a friend, because Clay's hurting, but being near him"—she gulped a deep breath—"it's difficult."

"Maybe more therapy would help you come to terms with his line of work."

"I don't think the rodeo is something I can ever come to terms with. I can't commit to a lifetime of worrying whether or not he'll come home every weekend."

"There's no guarantee any of us will see tomorrow no matter how tame our lifestyle." He pulled a small Bible from inside his jacket and flipped through the pages.

"Ecclesiastes 3:1–4 says, 'To every thing there is a season, and a time to every purpose under the heaven: a time to be born, and a time to die; a time to plant, and a time to pluck up that which is planted; a time to kill, and a time to heal; a time to break down, and a time to build up; a time to weep, and a time to laugh; a time to mourn, and a time to dance.'"

He ran his fingers over the leather cover. "Everyone has a time to die. Just because a man has a dangerous occupation, it doesn't mean he'll die young."

"Even if they do stupid, risky things?"

Brother Timothy chuckled. "If that were the case, no male would get past the teenage years."

"But don't you think if we're determined to take unnecessary chances, God might decide to shorten our time?"

"You think Mel died early because he tempted fate?"

Rayna shrugged. "Maybe."

"I don't believe in fate. I believe the only time God shortens a life span is if we know Him but don't live for Him. If we confess Him as Savior but live like the devil, then He might decide to call us home a bit early so we don't turn any of our brothers down the wrong road.

"I'm not saying every Christian who sins will die young. If that were the case, there wouldn't be any of us left." Brother Timothy smiled. "How're your folks?"

"Married and happier than I've ever seen them. They go to church every time the doors are open. I can't tell you how much we appreciate your help."

"I'm glad they're doing well." He patted her shoulder. "Right now we're mourning and weeping, but we need to get back to the laughing and dancing. I'll pray for you and Clay."

"Thank you. See you at the funeral."

❧

At the large church the Gentrys attended, visitation was surreal. People laughed and told stories, while Mel's body lay in his casket. Even in the most trying of times, God blessed the grieving with good memories.

Seated on a navy blue pew, Lacie looked pale and tired. Yet she greeted each visitor and listened to every story with a strained smile pasted on her face. Occasionally, a shared tale touched her heart and the smile reached her eyes. Her family and Clay kept close watch for the tiniest crack in her composure, ready with a shoulder or a hug.

The next day the funeral looked like a dramatic rodeo. Cowboys and cowgirls dressed in black made up most of the attendees. Lacie had insisted Clay and Rayna sit in the family section. It seemed right for Clay to be there, but not Rayna. Instead, she sat with some of the women she'd met at the few rodeos she'd attended. Natalie kept her distance. Suited Rayna just fine.

The pastor celebrated Mel's life and the legacy left behind. He outlined the plan of salvation and urged unbelievers to consider their destiny. Heaven or hell? From what little Rayna knew of Mel, she felt he'd be pleased. Through his death, maybe someone would come to know Christ.

At the close of the service, the mourners filed out. A man using a cane seemed familiar. The woman with him did, too. The last time she'd seen them, he'd been in a wheelchair.

She'd ridden with Clay, so she headed toward the back where the family would exit. At the side of the building, she saw Kendra. The usually pulled-together career woman seemed distracted.

"Hey Kendra, what are you doing here?"

"I came with Wyatt Marshall. We're dating."

Rayna had met Wyatt at the rodeo. *Dating a cowboy, huh?* She bit her tongue, remembering Kendra's numerous jokes during the ad campaign.

"You okay?"

"Sure. Why wouldn't I be?" Kendra's voice quivered.

Maybe she'd gotten to know Mel and Lacie well.

"There's Wyatt." Kendra headed in his direction.

"Are you going to the cemetery?"

"I hope not. I've had about all the grief I can stand." Kendra hurried to meet Wyatt and they exited.

❧

Rayna and Clay stayed at the cemetery until Lacie could bring herself to leave. The gray March day fit the occasion.

Back at the Gentry house, a few friends and family gathered. Thank goodness Star planned to stay for a few weeks. On the agenda, moving Mel's things into an extra closet. Rayna promised to help. When she and Clay left that evening, they both felt at ease leaving their friend in good hands.

As he opened the truck door for her, he winced and grabbed his shoulder.

"You've hurt it again?"

He nodded. "I'm having surgery at the end of the season."

Closing her eyes, she tried to fathom such stupidity. "Okay, I'll bite. Why not now?"

"You know why. I'd miss too much of the season."

"If you'd had surgery when the injury initially occurred, like your doctor recommended, you'd be healed by now. I can get my own door." She climbed into the truck and slammed her door shut. "Do I need to open yours, too?"

"No. I've got a good arm left. I can get them both." He jerked his open, climbed in, and slammed it behind him.

The ride back to the ranch echoed with silence.

He pulled into the familiar drive and parked by her car. "I guess this is the end of the line. I won't be seeing you again."

"I think that's best."

"How can it be best, Rayna? We love each other. How can two people—who should be two halves of a whole—living separate lives be best?"

fourteen

Rayna tried to swallow the large lump in her throat.

Clay sighed. "If it makes any difference, there's a reason I'm so determined to make the Cinch finale again. I'm dedicating my season to Mel. I'd like to honor his memory with a win, not with surgery and fizzling out."

Rayna's vision blurred. "That's very noble. I'm sure it means a lot to Lacie."

"It sure would mean a lot to me if you could stick around."

Shaking her head, she opened the truck door. "I can't." She slid out and hurried to her car.

⁂

Friday after work, Rayna parked by Clay's truck in Lacie's drive. She closed her eyes, took a deep breath, and got out. Three days since she'd seen him last. Why did he have to be here? Why had she promised to help with the closet? The breeze blew her hair into a tangle. *Great, the windblown look.*

Trying to smooth it back into some semblance of order, she squared her shoulders and rang the bell.

He answered. Green eyes widened. "Hey."

Why did he have to look so good? "I promised to help Lacie and Star with the closet."

"I'm working on the crib. They bought it a few weeks back and didn't get around to putting it together. I thought having some friends help might take the sting out."

"Shouldn't you be at the rodeo by now?"

"I'm leaving as soon as I get this project done."

"Does she know about you dedicating your season to Mel?"

"Cried. That's pretty much what she does these days. Mom said grief and hormones are a double whammy."

"I've heard pregnant women's emotions get all out of whack. She's got a lot on her." Eager to escape his presence,

149

Rayna hurried to Lacie's bedroom.

Star knelt in the closet doorway while Lacie sat on the bed clutching one of Mel's shirts to her nose.

Rayna's eyes burned, and she blinked several times. *Lord, I don't want to end up like that. Strip all traces of Clay Warren from my heart. Help me to heal. Surely there's someone out there with a harmless occupation.*

What was she thinking? Until Clay, she'd never realized she wanted anyone to share her life with.

Lacie's tear-brightened eyes radiated pain. "I must look like a ninny sitting here smelling his clothes."

"No, you don't."

"I don't want anything washed, just moved into the other closet. That way, every time I get dressed, I don't have to see his clothes. But when I want to, I can visit them. Silly, huh?"

A memory stole Rayna's breath for a moment. "I used to smell my mother's clothes after she left."

"Really?"

"It always helped." Rayna patted Lacie's shoulder.

Clay filled the doorway. "Crib's done. Wanna come see?"

Lacie's eyes closed.

"Maybe later," Star whispered.

"I wanna see it." Lacie stood. "I just wish Mel could."

Clay put his arm around the petite blond. Together, they walked across the hall. With a glimpse of the crib Mel would never see, fresh tears assaulted Lacie.

"Maybe this wasn't a good idea." Star linked arms with Lacie. "Let's go back to your room."

"No. I like being here." Lacie clung to Clay until she calmed. "Aren't you supposed to be at the rodeo, cowboy?"

"I've got time."

"I don't want you driving too fast. Go do Mel proud."

Clay kissed her forehead. "I will."

"And be careful." Lacie pointed a red fingernail in his face.

"I will." He glanced at Rayna and turned to go.

"Okay, I'm taking another load. Be back in a sec." Star exited, her arms piled high with western shirts.

Rayna stepped into the closet. "Does everything go?"

"Yeah." Lacie sniffled. "You know, I wouldn't give up a single second of our lives together. Even though it ended too soon, I'd marry Mel and suffer through every rodeo all over again. Even the final one. He was gone in an instant, but the nanosecond before that, he knew I was there supporting him."

Methodically, Rayna pulled clothes from the rack.

❧

Clay couldn't manage to take his eyes off Rayna. A whole week had passed since he'd last seen her. Seemed like years.

Dressed in paint-spattered jeans and T-shirt, with her hair pulled into a high ponytail, she was way too cute. When Lacie's friends had decided to paint the nursery, he didn't think Rayna would chance running into him again. Yet she did.

She straightened a corner of the drop cloth with her foot. "We need more paintbrushes."

"There's some on the kitchen table."

Rayna left to get them, and his heartbeat slowed.

"You know"—his mom propped her hands on her hips—"Lacie shouldn't be here."

"Why?" Clay poured pastel green paint in a roller pan. "I thought it might cheer her up, getting the nursery ready."

"Fumes. Pregnant women aren't supposed to breathe paint fumes. It's bad for the baby."

"How am I supposed to know these things?"

"We need to get her out of the house, but it's a bit nippy for sitting on the porch." Mama lined blue tape on the window facing.

Rayna returned with four brushes.

Tapping her chin with a forefinger, Mama turned toward her. "I've got it. You and Clay take Lacie out for the day."

Rayna's eyes widened. "Why?"

"Paint fumes are bad for the baby." Mama and Clay echoed each other.

Her hand flew to her mouth. "I didn't know that. We have to get her out of here."

"Okay, but where? Maybe the ranch?"

"I don't know. Let's just go."

Fifteen minutes later, they piled in his truck with Rayna in the middle. Her leg brushed his, and she jerked away.

Clay swallowed hard. He should have stayed at the house and let Rayna occupy Lacie. But in the rush to get the baby away from the fumes, he'd fallen into Mama's trap. A day spent with the woman he loved but couldn't have.

"Where are we going?" Lacie asked.

"I have no clue." Clay started the engine. "Away from fumes."

"We could go shopping for the baby." Rayna tugged her hair loose and pushed it back over her shoulders.

Silky strands of spun copper brushed his cheek, giving Clay the urge to run his fingers through it.

"My heart's not in it without Mel." Lacie adjusted her seat belt around the baby. "Don't you have a rodeo tonight?"

Rayna's jaw clenched.

Clay nodded.

"Breakfast at the ranch?" Rayna adjusted her shoulder strap.

"I guess I should feed the baby better. Fruit would be nice."

"Fruit it is." Clay turned toward the interstate. "Lacie, how about you stay there while we go back and paint?"

"Sounds fine, but I'd like to go to the rodeo tonight."

Had he heard Lacie right? "There's no need in that."

"Do you have any idea how long it's been since I missed a rodeo? It felt odd not going the last few weekends."

"I guess if that's what you want to do, you can go with me."

Arms crossed over her chest, Rayna didn't say a word.

Some way, he had to narrow the divide between them.

❧

That evening, with the nursery painted, Rayna couldn't wait to put some distance between her and Clay. She headed straight for her car as Ty helped Lacie out of his truck.

"Where's Clay?" Ty tipped his hat.

"Moving the furniture in. We opened all the windows to air out the house."

"I'll go help." Ty hurried inside.

"I hope," Lacie whispered, "you didn't tell Star where I'm going tonight."

"No."

"Good. She's leaving in the morning. She'd call Mama and Daddy. They'd all be upset and want me to move back to San Antonio with them."

"Won't they catch on?"

"I'll just say I'm visiting a friend. I won't have to lie, and they're not used to a rodeo every weekend."

"Are you sure you want to go?"

The pretty blond nodded. "For years I fought the rodeo with everything in me. Now it seems odd not to go. I think I'll feel closer to Mel there."

"I guess that makes sense."

"Now, I don't mean to pry, but you're missing out on time you could be spending with the man you love. Are you sure you and Clay can't work things out?"

"I can't do it, Lacie. I love him too much to wait around for him to get hurt. Or worse."

"I understand. I really do. More than most women could. But what if Clay died tonight?"

"Oh, don't even say that." Her heart gave a painful jolt.

"I know it's a horrible thought, but think about it. Would you hurt just as bad as if you were still together? Maybe even worse? Would you regret all this time apart? Wouldn't you rather wring out every possible second available to spend with him? Just think about it."

⋙

Rayna slowed the car as she neared Lacie's house. So far, the baby had been shy, not revealing his or her sex. With another ultrasound scheduled, Lacie wanted someone to share the occasion with and had set up an appointment on her clinic's late night to accommodate Rayna's workday.

Pulling in the drive, she frowned. Clay's truck. Lacie hadn't said anything about him.

He answered the door, looking better than any man she'd

ever seen. Why did he have to be so easy on the eyes?

"Hey there. I originally couldn't go 'cuz I had a horse training session, but Dad covered for me so I could surprise Lacie."

And me.

Lacie stepped up beside him.

He draped his arm around the mom-to-be's shoulders. "Missing Junior's revealing, it just didn't sit well."

"I hope he feels like revealing." Lacie's eyes shone. "Are we ready?"

At the doctor's office, women in various stages of pregnancy walked or waddled.

A nurse ushered Lacie back to lie on a table. "You've got one stubborn baby, Mrs. Gentry. I can't believe we haven't been able to determine the sex at this late stage."

"Like his daddy." Lacie patted her stomach. "Stubborn as a mule."

Rayna had never before seen an ultrasound. Apparently Clay hadn't either. She'd never seen him uneasy, until now.

"She's not gonna have to. . .uh. . .disrobe or nothing?"

"Clay Warren, do you think I would've let you come back here if I was gonna have to get naked?"

"Now, this will be cold." The technician pulled Lacie's shirt up and rubbed a gel-looking substance on her rounded belly. "Watch the screen."

All eyes were glued to the monitor.

A blurred image appeared then cleared.

"Is that supposed to be a baby?" Clay asked.

The technician laughed and moved a pointer on the screen. "Right here is the side of a leg and foot. The baby is lying on its side and being difficult as usual. Come on, baby, roll over. Spread those legs."

A perfect little foot kicked and squirmed. "Can you feel that?"

"He delivers some powerful wallops at times."

Clay lapsed into silence.

"Come on, baby, roll over," Lacie coaxed as the baby changed position.

"Now, there's the stomach." The technician moved the pointer farther down. "And there's. . . Congratulations, Lacie, you've got a boy."

"Really?" Clay asked.

"Right there's the evidence." Lacie couldn't talk anymore as tears streamed down her face.

❧

Rayna tried to bypass Clay as she left Lacie's house. If only seeing him would get less painful. But it didn't.

He fell into stride at her side. "That was pretty cool. I mean, I knew there was a baby in there, but seeing it. Wow."

"I wish Mel could be here with her."

"Me, too. Don't get me wrong. I don't believe all that mumbo jumbo about people watching from heaven. If they were all up there watching, how could there be no tears in heaven? But for stuff like this, maybe God pulls back a curtain."

"It's a nice thought."

"I don't want to miss out on that. I want to see my baby, feel its movements, see it born." He grabbed her hand and pulled her into his arms. "I want to marry you. I want to have children with you. Couldn't we make things work, Rayna?"

She could imagine watching their baby on the screen.

"Ow." He released her and grabbed his shoulder. "Sorry, wrong shoulder. Here, try this other one."

She jerked away with a world-weary sigh.

His cell phone rang, and he dug it from his pocket. "Hello? Hey Gabby. She's right here. Sure." He closed the phone, a worried look on his face. "Wyatt and Kendra were in a car accident."

She gasped. "Are they hurt?"

"Gabby called trying to find you."

Rayna dug her phone from her purse. Dead battery.

"She didn't know any details. I'll drive."

❧

Kendra met them in the emergency room, her eyes red-rimmed. "I think Wyatt's okay. They're checking him over."

"Are you all right?" Rayna hugged her. "Did anyone else get hurt?"

"I'm fine. And we didn't hit anyone else. We were celebrating Wyatt's birthday, and we both had too many drinks with dinner. It's a wonder we didn't kill ourselves and others."

Clay ran his hand through his hair. "What was he thinking?"

"He wasn't. Neither of us was. His blood alcohol was just under the legal radar."

"Here, sit down." Rayna put her arm around Kendra's shoulders.

"I saw my life flash before my eyes. And it wasn't pretty."

Rayna's eyes widened. "Maybe this is a wake-up call from God."

"I know you won't believe this, but that's what I was thinking."

Rayna glanced over Kendra's head at Clay.

"Come to church with us Sunday." Clay smoothed a hair away from Kendra's face.

"Okay."

Wow, that was easy.

"But I think I'd like to get some things straight now. If it's okay. I mean, do you have to be in church to get saved?"

"No." Rayna clasped her hand. "You can do that anywhere."

"Even if you're doing it 'cause you got scared out of your wits?"

"If you're sincere about it."

"You've told me a zillion times, but how does it go again?"

"Just admit to Jesus you're a sinner and that you need Him in your life. Ask for forgiveness of your sins. Do you want me to pray with you now?"

"I think I should do it." Kendra bowed her head. "Dear Lord, I know I'm a sinner, and I ask You to forgive me. I want to change. I want to be a different person. I need You to help me do that. Make me a better person. Clean up my past and help me to start a new life. I accept You in my life. I need Your guidance. I've made such a mess of things." Kendra peeked up at Rayna. "How's that?"

"Very good."

"Oops, I need to say amen or something, don't I? Sorry,

Lord, I'm new at this. Amen."

Rayna hugged her. "I'm so happy for you."

"The next step is to find a church home." Clay patted her arm. "You can still go to church with Rayna and me Sunday."

"I will. I promise."

"While y'all were praying, the doctor came out. Wyatt's fine." Clay winked.

"Oh thank goodness." Kendra covered her face with her hands.

"How about we take you home?" Rayna put her arm around her shoulders.

"Thanks, but I'd like to stay with Wyatt. You two go, and I'll see you Sunday. Maybe Wyatt will come, too."

❧

"That was awesome." Clay turned out of the hospital lot.

"It was. God is awesome." Rayna blew out a satisfied sigh. "All the time Gabby and I spent witnessing to Kendra, she never showed the slightest interest. In fact, at times, she got downright mad at us."

"But you kept at it. And all that time, God was tenderizing her heart. You won her over to Christ."

"I've never done that before. It felt great."

"Don't you think if God can turn someone like Kendra around, He could work things out for two people meant to be together?"

fifteen

"Please don't." A lump lodged in Rayna's throat.

"You talk about how stubborn I am. But you're one of the orneriest fillies I've ever known."

She put her finger against his lips, wishing she could silence him with a kiss instead. "I don't want to fight with you. Let's just pray about us. Okay?"

He nodded. "I'll pick you up for church Sunday."

"You roped me into that one, didn't you?"

"That's what you gotta do with ornery fillies sometimes. Besides, Mama's throwing Lacie a baby shower that afternoon and wants you to help."

"Anything for Lacie." Roped her right into spending half the day with him.

❧

In the kitchen, Rayna and Durlene stirred and baked while the men took charge of decorating the great room.

"It was nice meeting your friends this morning." Durlene dropped a spoon in the soapy-water-filled sink. "Clay said she got saved recently."

"I was surprised to find them ready and waiting when we arrived to pick them up. I thought she might chicken out, and I didn't think Wyatt would come." Had Wyatt spent the night with Kendra? Even if he had, God would convict Kendra on the changes needed in her life.

"I saw Brother Timothy talking with her after the service."

"Wyatt looked bored and out of place despite Clay's attempts at conversation."

"Maybe he'll come around. At least he heard the Gospel."

The door opened.

"Hey, I'm making a mess." Clay leaned against the door facing with a roll of tangled baby-blue crepe paper in each hand. "Maybe you can help."

"Rayna, I think the decorations need a woman's touch." Durlene stirred strawberries into the fruit salad.

Everyone must be in on the conspiracy to inflict Clay on her peace of mind. Rayna snatched one of the rolls from him and headed to the next room.

"Hey, what did I do?"

"You exist."

"You know, if you'd quit being so stubborn, my existing could be a good thing."

"Here. Tape this in that corner over there."

He climbed the step stool and followed her directions.

Backing away from him, she rotated the crepe paper. Ten minutes later, crisscrossed, curling streamers lined the ceiling.

"How'd you do that?"

Rayna shrugged and headed back toward the kitchen, but Clay blocked her path.

"What are you doing?"

"Trying to convince you we should be together."

His head lowered toward hers.

Turn away. But she couldn't will herself to do it.

Their lips met and a longing for life with him as his wife filled her soul.

"Hey." Ty's voice echoed down the hall.

They sprang apart.

"Our guest of honor has arrived."

Rayna took a quivery breath.

Ty opened the door and ushered Lacie inside. "Aren't you a pretty little mama."

"Thanks." Lacie positively glowed, though sadness lurked in her eyes. "Ooh, the decorations are pretty. Y'all shouldn't have gone to such trouble."

"Rayna whipped it together in minutes. How you feelin'?" Clay gave her a warm hug.

"Good. Really good."

"You're almost there."

"I want you to be there when he's born."

While Clay coughed, frowned, and muttered, Rayna tried to contain her laughter.

"I don't mean in my room. In the waiting room."

Clay mopped his forehead. "Just try to keep me away."

"We'd better git, son. More ladies'll be showing up anytime, and your mama said we had to skedaddle."

"Let's go make sure she doesn't need any more manpower; then we'll head out the back."

The two men disappeared down the hall, so similar in carriage, except for Ty's limp. Clay could be in the same condition in a few more years. A chill crawled over her skin.

"He gives you the shivers, huh?" Lacie nudged her with an elbow. "You need to marry him, you know?"

Rayna closed her eyes.

"I'd like to see y'all happy, and the only way that will happen is if you quit fighting it. Wouldn't you rather have however much time you can get with the man you love than nothing?"

"But I don't want to end up. . ."

"Like me? I know. But I'd rather have the memories with Mel and this little treasure." Lacie rubbed her stomach. "I think somebody's here."

Rayna looked out the window to see shower guests arriving and hurried to perform her hostess duties.

❧

A blessed day. Gabby and Adam's wedding day. Rayna waited in the back of the church with her friend. A stab of envy tightened her stomach. Over the years, she'd attended numerous weddings, but never before had she wished it were her own. With Clay.

The music began. "Ready?" she whispered.

Gabby giggled. "Way past."

Ushers pulled the double doors open, and Rayna, wearing yellow poof, stutter-stepped down the aisle. The pale color sapped her complexion. The ruffles and lace itched. The result: she was one big splotchy bridesmaid. If only she hadn't scratched at the neckline, her sensitive skin wouldn't have responded with hives. But it didn't matter anyway. Today was Gabby and Adam's day.

Halfway down the aisle, she saw him. Her rhythm faltered for a moment. Pasting a smile on her face, she stared straight ahead, thankful when she passed him.

She took her place at the front of the sanctuary and, careful to keep her gaze away from the guests, watched Kendra approach. A new Kendra. The jet-black hair with burgundy highlights had softened to a lovely, natural golden brown. The "Wedding March" punctuated the silence, and everyone stood as Gabby made her way down the aisle.

Adam couldn't take his eyes off his bride.

Rayna stole a quick glance. Her gaze met Clay's, then darted away.

Gabby's father, his features taut with emotion, performed his duty and took his seat.

The ceremony got under way. Rayna didn't hear anything the pastor said, not even any of the vows.

Kendra's finger dug into the middle of her back. "The ring," she whispered.

Rayna slid Adam's wedding band off her thumb just as Gabby turned to claim it.

After the couple exchanged rings, a love song played while they lit the unity candle. Closing her eyes, Rayna tried not to imagine her and Clay standing there gazing at each other.

At the close of the ceremony, the wedding party stood in the lobby as well-wishers hugged the happy couple. Clay advanced through the line. Typical black jeans, boots, and a tuxedo jacket. And typically, he looked great.

As he hugged Gabby, Rayna made a run for it and hid in a classroom.

❧

As guests filtered into the fellowship hall and the wedding party went back to the sanctuary for pictures, Clay turned to leave. He'd hoped to speak with Rayna. To be close to her, get a whiff of her maddening perfume, but she'd disappeared.

Her head popped out of a doorway.

He backed into an alcove, hoping she hadn't seen him.

Seconds later, she hurried toward the sanctuary.

"There you are."

She skidded to a halt with a little yelp.

"Sorry. I always seem to scare the wits out of you."

She turned toward him. Angry welts covered her face, shoulders, and arms.

He ran his fingertips over her cheek. "Hey, are you okay? Are you allergic to something?"

Her throat muscles constricted. "Lace makes me itch, and sometimes when I scratch, I get hives."

"Why didn't you tell Gabby when she picked it out?"

"It's her wedding day. She ought to be able to have her bridesmaids wear goofy dresses if she wants. Besides, I didn't think I'd break out over it. How bad is it?"

"Don't worry. You're still beautiful. Gabby was looking for you. I think they're taking pictures."

"Once they get a look at me, they may decide against it."

"It probably won't show. And even if it does, you already stole the bride's thunder by showing up." He traced her jawline. "I wish. . ."

"I'd better go." Gathering her skirts, she charged toward the sanctuary.

৯৯

By the following Saturday night, Rayna's hives had subsided. Each jolt the bareback horse inflicted on Clay forced her fingertips deeper into the well-worn knees of her jeans. Her knuckles turned white and she dug her long, perfectly manicured nails farther into her flesh.

Eight long seconds and it ended. Her self-torture eased. Clay successfully dismounted the horse and climbed the arena fence. Both knees stung with the prickling sensation of scrapes. *Long, slow breaths. Try to relax.*

How could a city girl, who adored everything that glittered, fall in love with a cowboy who swaggered into her world only seven months ago? Now here she sat at the Fort Worth Stockyards on unyielding aluminum seats. She must be crazy. Lacie's words had echoed in her head for weeks. *"You're missing out on time with the man you love."* Adam's wedding had only driven home the truth. Without Clay, her life was empty.

God had brought the perfect man into her life. A man who made her long for home and family. And she'd spent the last few months pushing him away. Because of fear.

"I thought that was you, Rayna. Long time, no see. At the arena, I mean."

She knew the voice, even before shielding her eyes to look up at its owner. Creating a halo effect, Lacie's bleached blond hair reflected the harsh rays of the fluorescent lights. Rayna jumped to her feet, throwing her arms around her very pregnant friend.

"Are you and Clay back tog—?"

"No. I only came for support."

"You should have let me know you were coming. I just happened to see you."

"I honestly didn't know I was until yesterday. I guess I missed the smell of manure." Rayna scrunched her nose.

"Such ambience." Lacie laughed. "But I don't think that's what you missed. Clay's in the lead. Only one more competition tonight."

The coming event turned Rayna's blood cold.

The smells, the sights, the sounds. Some of it had grown on her, especially the man who had drawn her here tonight. "Let's get something to drink."

Lacie agreed, and they stood then slowly made their way down the steps. "Does Clay know you're here?"

"No. I didn't want to sidetrack him, so I waited until things got under way. I got here in time to see the calf roping." It seemed so cruel to throw the helpless animals down and hog-tie them. Despite Clay's insistence that the calves weren't hurt, Rayna had never been convinced.

"Clay doesn't compete in steer roping anymore. He didn't think it was right to find a new partner." Sadness glowed in Lacie's eyes. "So what have you been doing with yourself?"

"Same old, same old. Working and more working. We just wrapped up a big ad campaign for Total Workout. It's a new exercise clothing line."

"Now let's not beat around the bush. This is Lacie you're talking to. He misses you. It broke Clay's heart when things didn't work out between you two. Broke your heart, too. You know it, and I know it."

She couldn't come up with an answer for that one and changed the subject. "You look good."

"You're surprised I'm here." Slim shoulders shrugged. "It still feels odd not to be, and since Clay's dedicated his season to Mel, I try to support him. And besides, being here, it always makes me feel closer to Mel." She ran her hand over her swollen abdomen.

"Only a matter of days to go."

"I can't wait." Lacie's eyes glistened. "I just wish. . ."

The teenage boy at the concession stand took their order.

Lacie pulled herself together to relay the latest rodeo news, and Rayna's mind wandered back to her first glimpse of the cowboy who had stolen her heart so completely.

"Ma'am. Ma'am!" The boy held a wax-coated paper cup toward her.

"Sorry." She took the iced tea, a taste she'd developed from spending time at the ranch. After paying, she and Lacie turned back toward the arena.

"Are you gonna stick around after the competition tonight? He'd love to see you. And the way you were straining your eyes earlier, you'd love a closer look at him as well."

"Ladies and Gentlemen," the announcer's voice boomed over the loudspeaker, "and now for our final event of the evening, the bull-riding competition." He named the lineup.

Rayna took several deep, cleansing breaths, trying not to listen. She gulped the iced tea, but too late, she heard Clay's name. He'd ride third. At least this sense of dread wouldn't last the entire event.

"We'd better get back. I still cross all my digits when Clay rides, and that takes a few minutes, especially since I can't see my toes." Lacie smiled and linked her arm through Rayna's. "We just have to place him in God's hands."

Unwanted visions and memories threatened to surface. Rayna stopped. "You go on. I can't watch."

"You're staying out here?"

In the lobby with no visibility. Just the way Rayna wanted it. Listening to the events unfold would be bad enough.

Her stomach knotted, her mouth went dry, and bile rose to the back of her throat. Unable to form words, she nodded.

"You sure? Wouldn't you rather sit with me?"

Swallowing hard, Rayna forced the bitter taste down. "I can't. I'll be fine right here."

"Okay, but don't you leave without saying good-bye." With a shrug, Lacie hugged Rayna. "And even after we say good-bye, let's not be strangers. You call me."

"I will." Rayna managed a smile.

"And remember what I said about Clay. He really misses you." Lacie wagged a crimson fingernail. Another quick hug, and she walked away.

Clay's ride would be over soon. She'd never promised to stay, only that she'd call.

Oh why had she come? Because she couldn't stay away. Mel's death, Lacie's loneliness, her parents' happiness, and Adam's wedding had all ganged up on her. She wanted to wring out whatever time she could have with Clay.

Previous rides Rayna witnessed played over in her memory until the announcer's voice lassoed her back to the present.

"Next up, Clay Warren riding Rage."

sixteen

Rayna gasped.

"Yes, Ladies and Gentlemen, the same bull that almost sent Clay Warren to meet his Maker a few months ago. That's the luck of the draw."

She couldn't stay, not even just to listen. Gasping and stumbling, Rayna bolted for the door. April's warm evening air smothered her chest, driving the breath from her lungs.

"Ladies and Gentlemen, the moment we've all been waiting for. Can Clay Warren tame Rage? Will it be man or beast in this raging rematch?"

Only yards from her car, she stopped. Throughout every fiber of her being, she yearned to flee but couldn't. Not until she knew whether or not he'd be okay. She pulled out her inhaler, took two puffs, and made a mad dash across the parking lot.

Back to the arena. She had to get inside to see. See the man she loved more than life. The man she had to have, rodeo or not.

The guard scanned her ticket stub and let her pass.

She gasped for breath. A vise tightened around her heart as she hurried through the lobby. Clay tossed about like a rag doll. Each jolt sent a shock wave through his entire body. Time stood still. Surely the clock had malfunctioned.

In Your hands, Lord. His life, our love, our future. In Your hands. The pressure in her chest eased. A sense of peace flowed over her.

The buzzer sounded, and she exhaled.

Clay nimbly jumped from Rage's back and the barrel man ran to divert the rust-colored bull's attention. Both men made it to safety. The bullfighters teased and coaxed until the bull exited the arena.

Her breath came more easily. The constriction of her chest

eased as she bolted toward the cowboy-congested bucking chutes. Clay perched on the fence with his back toward her as a rock song blared from the speakers.

Unconcerned with onlookers, she cupped her hands around her mouth and screamed his name. "Clay!"

He turned and searched the crowd.

Waving both arms in the air, she called again, "Clay!"

He saw her then. Disbelief played across his handsome features, and he squinted as if not trusting his eyesight. He smiled. His green eyes brightened as he jumped from his perch atop the fence and ran toward her.

She flew into his arms, and he spun her around until she was dizzy before gently setting her down. They kissed long and hard, the way she'd wanted to for months, before finally coming up for air.

Whoops and whistles echoed from the cowboys surrounding the chutes.

Warmth crept up her neck as she inhaled deeply the heady mixture of sweat and dust that clung to him.

He led her to the separate lobby near the back exit. "How long you been here, pretty lady?"

"I got here just in time to see some of the guys torturing those poor calves." She smiled up at him.

He leaned his forehead against hers. "You're really here. I never thought I'd lay eyes on you again at a rodeo." He stiffened and released her.

The gulf between them widened.

Turning his attention to kicking at a clod of dirt someone had tracked in, he drawled, "What brings you here?"

"You. I love you."

Surprise shone in his eyes. "And I love you, but we're as different as a mule and an Arabian."

She laughed. She'd missed his cowboyisms. "We'll work it out."

"I can't quit."

"I know." She closed her eyes.

"My ride wasn't good enough. I'll probably get second."

"You've got the rest of the season. And there's always next year."

His knuckles gently grazed her cheek as he searched her eyes. "You gonna be here next year?"

Time for the city girl to take the bull by the horns. "Will you marry me?"

"Yee-haaa!" He threw his hat in the air and spun her around again. "Ow, ow, ow. Wrong shoulder." He set her down.

A worried frown drew his brows together. "Now don't get mad. I'm having surgery at the end of this season."

She traced his jaw with her fingertips. "And I'll be there to make sure you do."

❧

Clay stepped inside the ranch house.

"You look bull whipped." Mama patted his cheek. "Your daddy's in the den. I'll get you a glass of tea."

"Thanks, Mama." He ambled down the hall.

Dad sat on the couch, and Clay sank into an oversized recliner across from him.

"Rayna showed up tonight. She proposed."

"Has she come to terms with the rodeo?"

"Prayed her way through it."

"I knew that girl was a smart one." Dad propped his feet on the coffee table. "I reckon you were smart and said yes."

"Oh yeah."

Dad took a swig of his coffee. "You know, son, I should have told you something a long time ago."

Clay frowned. "What?"

"Your mama and me raised you at the rodeo. It was our life, and that's the way we both wanted it. Your mama was practically born and raised at the rodeo, and it never bothered her. I mean, she worries, but nothing she can't handle."

"Rayna's different. She says I'm worth it, but I worry about the stress I cause her."

"Me, too, son. Me, too." Dad gulped more coffee. "You probably feel a certain amount of pressure to follow in my footsteps."

Clay's chest tightened. Words escaped him.

"You had a great season last year, son." Dad leaned forward. "I don't want you to ever feel like there's a shadow you have to live up to. You're your own man. Just because I won four Texas Circuit Finals and National Circuit Finals doesn't mean you have to. If you get tired of the road, tired of traveling, tired of stressing the woman you love, you can quit. With my blessing."

Footsteps sounded in the hall.

"Here we are." Mama entered the room and handed Clay a glass. "Iced tea for one tired three-time CBR World Champ."

The phone rang.

"Late for anybody to be calling." Dad scooped up the handset. "Warren Dude Ranch."

He covered the mouthpiece and grinned. "Lacie's in labor."

❧

Clay squeezed Rayna's hand as they waited for their first glimpse of little Mel.

The night had been dreamlike. Had Rayna really proposed to this hunk of a cowboy? Clay brought out a side of her she didn't recognize.

They'd seen Lacie, pain etched on her face, for a moment before she went into the birthing room. Long enough for Rayna to decide that when the time came, there would be nothing natural about her having a baby. She wanted drugs—and lots of them.

Finally, Star stepped out of Lacie's room and gestured them in.

Lacie sat in her bed with a tiny bundle in her arms.

Rayna couldn't take her eyes off the contented mother and child. A glance at Clay proved he couldn't either.

A few minutes later, Clay and Rayna said their good-byes and left the family alone.

"Wow." Clay took her hand as they walked out into the starlit night.

"Yeah."

"If only Mel were here. It's a shame."

She laid her head against his shoulder.

❧

May 25. Rayna spent the morning of her wedding day in a flurry of activity. Back at the apartment with her hair piled high with curls and soft tendrils trailing down her neck, she packed the last of her things.

An eternity with the man she loved stretched before her. And rodeos. Lots of them, and she'd attend each event, praying them both through it, supporting the man she loved.

And thankfully, after his end-of-the-season surgery, for three glorious months she wouldn't have to worry about him. Oh, she knew he'd probably push things and insist on competing before his doctor released him, even though it would cut his recovery time short. But they'd cross that divide when they came to it. And they'd work it out.

She checked her watch. In a few hours, she'd walk down the aisle and claim her cowboy. Lacie would serve as bridesmaid with Kendra, while Gabby would be matron of honor. Rayna had considered making them wear lace and organza but couldn't bring herself to do it. Instead, she chose teal-green satin.

In his father's stead, little Mel would be best man, while Ty and Stetson, the new rodeo clown—bullfighter—would serve as groomsmen. Kendra and Wyatt were still dating. Though he'd made no decision for Christ, he still attended church with her.

Rayna scanned the empty apartment. Some of her furniture had sold, and what she'd kept had already been moved to the ranch. Integrating her modern pieces with the rodeo look would be a challenge. But fun.

Strange. The condo had always been empty, but she'd never noticed until she met Clay. It was hard to imagine the lifestyle she'd thought she wanted, a career and a town house, with no husband or children. Thankfully, God had intervened for her.

A knock sounded at the door.

"Who is it?"

"A very eager groom."

"What are you doing here?" She opened the door.

Clay flashed a mischievous grin. "I came to steal the bride away for a little while."

"But we're not supposed to see each other before the wedding."

He cocked an eyebrow. "Are you superstitious?"

"No."

"What are we waiting for?"

"Where are we going?"

"Can't tell you. I've got a wedding present for you."

Intrigued, she wavered. "We have to be at the church soon."

"Trust me. I'll make sure we don't miss our wedding."

"Okay, carry the dress, but no peeking. You're not seeing it until I walk down the aisle."

"Scout's honor." He saluted with a wink and draped the long, vinyl zippered bag over his arm.

☙

"You can uncover your eyes now." Clay's drawl close to her ear sent shivers over her.

Rayna moved her hands away from her face. The Cowtown Coliseum in Fort Worth? Her blood boiled. "You're in a rodeo? Today!"

"Of course not. Settle down. You'll like this."

Instead of the usual trucks and horse trailers, cars jammed the back lot, along with several news vans.

"What's going on?"

"Come on and you'll see. Let's hurry. We've got a wedding to get to."

She took his hand and walked inside.

"There you are." Billy Thornton, Clay's publicist, looked relieved. "I thought you was gonna be late for your own press conference."

"Press conference?" Oh, he'd signed with CWW for next year. She was proud of him, but it seemed an odd wedding gift.

"Play your cards right, and there'll still be contracts and

endorsements." Billy clapped Clay on the back.

Rayna frowned as Billy led them through the lobby and into the Texas Rodeo Cowboy Hall of Fame. Why wouldn't there be contracts and endorsements?

As soon as Clay became visible to the crowd, numerous flashes went off and reporters jockeyed with questions.

"Ladies and Gentlemen." Billy held up both hands, trying to hush the crowd. "Thank you all for coming today. Mr. Warren has an announcement he'd like to make."

Clay tucked Rayna's hand into the crook of his arm.

"I'll just stay in the background." She tried to pull away.

"I want you by my side."

Her stomach knotted.

"Come on. You don't have to say a word. Just look pretty, and you don't have to do anything to do that." He winked.

She managed to dislodge her feet and walk to the microphone with him.

"Hey folks, thanks for coming. As everyone knows, it's been a difficult year for me. We lost a good man and the best friend I ever had in Mel Gentry. I dedicated my season in honor of his memory, and I'm glad that with God's help, so far, I'm doing him proud."

Tears filled Rayna's eyes as applause erupted.

Clay waited until the crowd quieted. "This is my fiancée, Rayna Landers. She's been by my side through most of the last year, and it's become apparent to me in recent months that there are more important things than the rodeo."

Rayna gasped.

He turned toward her.

"Are you sure?" she mouthed.

He responded with a definite nod. "I've decided to retire. At the end of this season, win or lose, I'm officially retired."

Hushed muttering arose from the crowd.

"Now I'm sure you have lots of questions, but Rayna and I have somewhere important to be, so Billy here will answer for me. I just want to say thanks to all the fans, and I'll miss you." With a wave, he winked at the crowd then ushered

Rayna to the lobby.

Questions erupted from the floor.

"Now rest assured," Billy said, "that our CBR World Champ will be happy to entertain endorsement offers after his contract with CWW expires at the end of the year."

They hurried to the back exit. In the separate lobby, Rayna stopped.

"Don't you think we'd better get to the church?"

"Are you sure about this?"

He cupped her face in his hands. "I've never been so positive about anything."

"You don't think you'll miss the rodeo? I don't want you to do this for me."

"You did awhile back."

"I guess I've done some soul-searching since then. It's not fair for you to give up something you love because of me. You'll end up resenting me, and I don't want that. I'm fine with the rodeo." She winced. "And I'm trusting God with our future. Everyone has a time to die, whether they ride bulls for a living or not."

"True." He kissed her forehead. "But I don't want to miss out on loving you. Not for a second. And because I love you, I don't want to spend time away from you traveling. I'm tired of the road and tired of causing you worry and torment. And I'm ready for this. Mel's death proved to me the rodeo isn't everything. Having a normal life, mundane and unexciting, sleeping with a wife you adore every night and raising kids together, that's what I want."

"What if you get bored?"

"Rayna Landers—soon to be Rayna Warren—you can be a lot of things, but never boring."

Her vision blurred. "You're sure about this."

"This shoulder injury and little Mel's birth helped the decision along. I want to be able to pick up our kids and toss them in the air. My dad could never do that. And I never wanted to outdo Dad. Three or four titles are plenty."

She gently pressed her palm against his bad shoulder.

"You're still having surgery."

"Right after I win the world title again."

"What if you don't win the title?"

"Either way, my heart's just not in another season." He sealed the deal with a toe-curling kiss.

When their lips parted, she had to cling to him just to stand up.

"Remember that vacation you never booked at the ranch?"

"Yeah."

"I'm willing to give you lifetime room and board." He winked.

She giggled. "Only until we build our cabin in the woods."

"I thought you didn't want to live anywhere near the woods."

"It depends. Is there a cowboy included with the cabin in the woods?"

"Will just any cowboy do?"

She pressed her cheek against his heartbeat. "Only the most perfect cowboy in Texas will do."

Her cowboy.

A Letter To Our Readers

Dear Reader:

In order that we might better contribute to your reading enjoyment, we would appreciate your taking a few minutes to respond to the following questions. We welcome your comments and read each form and letter we receive. When completed, please return to the following:

Fiction Editor
Heartsong Presents
PO Box 719
Uhrichsville, Ohio 44683

1. Did you enjoy reading *Rodeo Dust* by Shannon Taylor Vannatter?
   ❏ Very much! I would like to see more books by this author!
   ❏ Moderately. I would have enjoyed it more if

   _____

   _____

   _____

2. Are you a member of **Heartsong Presents**? ❏ Yes ❏ No
   If no, where did you purchase this book? _____

   _____

3. How would you rate, on a scale from 1 (poor) to 5 (superior), the cover design? _____

4. On a scale from 1 (poor) to 10 (superior), please rate the following elements.

   ____ Heroine   ____ Plot
   ____ Hero   ____ Inspirational theme
   ____ Setting   ____ Secondary characters

5. These characters were special because? _____

_____

_____

6. How has this book inspired your life? _____

_____

_____

7. What settings would you like to see covered in future
   Heartsong Presents books? _____

_____

_____

8. What are some inspirational themes you would like to see
   treated in future books? _____

_____

_____

9. Would you be interested in reading other **Heartsong
   Presents** titles?   ❏ Yes   ❏ No

10. Please check your age range:
    ❏ Under 18   ❏ 18-24
    ❏ 25-34   ❏ 35-45
    ❏ 46-55   ❏ Over 55

Name _____

Occupation _____

Address _____

City, State, Zip _____

E-mail _____